Author's Note:

This is a work of fiction. All names, characters, places,
and events are the work of the author's imagination. Any
resemblance to real persons, places, or events is
coincidental.

ISBN: 9798866567171

Cover Design by Joanne M.

First printing edition 2023

After the Syzygy

By J.D Sanderson

2036

"Okay, so what the hell am I looking at here?"

"Are you seriously asking me to explain it to you?"

"No, Gene, I'm not seriously asking you to explain it to me. I know what it is. I just want to know why you're showing it to me before my meeting this morning."

"Because this didn't pop into my inbox this morning as a preview. They weren't pressing us for a comment. This page is live on the internet right now."

George Gracie froze before his coffee cup could reach his mouth. "I hope to God you're screwing with me. It's too early for jokes." He looked through the rims of his glasses as Gene McCabe, the White House Communications Director, shook his head.

"Afraid not. Someone's got to tell POTUS, now, because in about 30 seconds, our switchboards are going to light up like a Christmas tree."

"Shit. Yes. We'd better get to her."

"Sounds like a job for the Chief of Staff."

"I said it was too early for jokes." George sipped his coffee as he ran his hands through his white hair.

"You've known her longer than any of us, George. It should come from you."

"And what the hell would you like me to lead with, Gene? 'Hey, Madame President? The biggest discovery in the history of humanity was somehow leaked to the press in an election year?'"

"Well, that's better than anything I could come up with right now."

"How did you find this?" George asked.

"One of the interns handed it to me. He was trying to find some good news online." Gene shook his head and reached for his water bottle.

"What'd you tell him?"

"I told him that if he so much as breathed in the direction of another human being, I'd staple his tongue to his forehead," Gene whispered as a pair of staffers walked by on their way to the West Wing.

The pair stared at the website on the small tablet. There were several screenshots of email messages on display throughout the article. George winced as he saw his email signature at the end of one of the messages. He rolled his eyes as Gene scrolled down to reveal several of the classified images.

His angry train of thought was interrupted by a tap on the shoulder from White House Press Secretary Martea Salazar. He had messaged her five minutes earlier to meet him by his office. The dark tight curls she usually kept pinned and out of the way were left hanging.

"Morning, Martea," George said.

"Jesus, George. You might as well be drawing the circles under your eyes with a marker," she chuckled. "This was supposed to be my first day off in weeks. I was just dropping off a few notes for someone when you messaged me. What's up?"

George held up the tablet for her.

"Oh, God," Martea said. She took a deep breath in, hoping her eye would refrain from twitching. "How much did they publish?"

"Twenty-five emails. Pretty much everything of note," Gene replied.

The senior White House staff had known about it for two weeks. Someone, somehow managed to break into a government email account, leading to a bundle of top-secret files being copied. As of today, it was still unknown if the breach was committed by someone inside, or if it was a sophisticated hack.

"This is the fourth major leak in a year," Martea said, jotting down some notes on her mobile. "Her polls are going to drop below forty percent."

"I think we're beyond that," Gene snipped. He looked over to a screen on the wall that monitored the major news networks. So far, none of them had gone live with the leaked files. "When this gets out, it's going to cause a complete panic."

"Have you told her yet?" Martea asked.

"Nope," Gene said. "She thought the fact nothing broke yet was a good sign. We were hoping that we just might have skated and were in the clear."

"This was supposed to be locked down, kept quiet, and buried in a shallow grave until we got our partners in the international community on board," Martea whispered. "Only three other countries have any knowledge of this."

"Yeah, that's what George's email on page two says," Gene muttered, waving the tablet in front of their faces. "You should frame it, George. It would look great above your desk!"

"I'm going to print them out, wad them up, and stuff them down the throat of whoever leaked this," George said.

"Jesus Christ, lower your voices!" Martea kept her voice to a harsh whisper. "Let's get in there and tell her now!"

The trio turned and made their way down the hallway toward the Oval Office, careful not to say anything as their feet shuffled across the well-worn gray carpet. While this part of the White House was always buzzing with activity, this new, low murmur somehow felt decidedly louder. More and more staffers were whispering as they looked down at their mobiles, wristcoms, or monitors.

"Oh, God," Gene muttered.

"Damn, damn, damn! So much for my time off," Martea said, trying her best to look calm. She tugged on Gene's sleeve as a familiar musical sting broke out on one of the nearby monitors. They looked on in horror as one of the evening news anchors broke in to make a special announcement.

"Good morning. We're coming to you live with a stunning report. Leaked communications from inside President Candace Park's White House. These disturbing documents have made it to several news sites over the last hour–"

"Oh hell," Gene blurted. "Run!"

Gene, George, and Martea picked up the pace on the way to the Oval Office. George found himself regretting the large pizza and soda he had consumed the previous night. It was work to keep up with his younger colleagues.

They all stopped as another anchor from a competing news channel on the monitor right outside the Oval Office, watching in horror as the screenshot of George's emails was replaced by one of the digital images first received at the Square Kilometer Array three months earlier.

The 1420 MHz signal had been caught by a team of observers in the middle of the night, arriving in seven distinct bursts, repeating after the final part. It contained text, sounds, and images, one of which was now being shown to the entire world.

Gene lowered his forehead into his hand as the anchor continued to speak. The images from George's emails were discovered within the sixth and seventh signal bursts by team members in Japan. The message's content had completely baffled everyone who reviewed it. The top experts from the United States, Japan, Australia, and the United Kingdom were unable to decipher anything specific meaning or intent from what they believed to be text. The digital images were equally hard to understand with no common frame of reference.

Together the four countries locked in and monitored the signal for days before it faded. It was a miracle that an amateur astronomer had not caught the signal and recorded it. An agreement was made on the spot to continue working together in total secrecy. The leaders of all four nations were hoping to decipher the signal before bringing in the rest of the international community. Now it was too late.

Gene and George looked at one another as they heard the newscast come from inside the Oval Office. George peeked inside, seeing a look on President Park's face that could have burned through the Resolute desk.

Gene tried his best not to slam his hand into the wall as one of the news anchors introduced to a top Harvard astrophysicist to speculate if the strange outline contained in one of the emails was indeed displaying an alien lifeform.

**

George walked into Gene's office to find his old friend's head in his hands. Martea was sitting on his couch with a mobile in each hand, checking for reactions from the public.

5

"It was a good speech, Gene," George said, sitting in an empty chair. "One of the better ones Candace has delivered. And I'll bet it goes over well with the public!"

"I agree. It was a nice way to end the longest twelve hours in history," Martea added.

The story spread like wildfire, with news agencies across the globe picking it up. President Park had spent the better part of six hours on the phone with world leaders, apologizing to those that were left out, and groveling to those that were in the loop for not telling them about the leak sooner.

George turned to look at Martea. "So, how is it going over?"

"So far it's about fifty-fifty," Martea said.

"And that means?"

"Roughly fifty percent of the traffic online is expressing outrage that this came out through a leak rather than a formal address from the president. The other fifty percent is chattering about conspiracy theories and the coming apocalypse. The disinformation farms are pumping out posts faster than I can track."

"There! See?" George turned back to Gene. "It went over well!"

"Shut up, George," Gene said, eliciting a laugh from his friend. He was still looking down at his desk. Martea glared over to the Chief of Staff.

"This isn't funny," she said. "There's a reason this shit was supposed to be kept under wraps. Information like this needs to be analyzed, studied, and peer-reviewed before it can be sanitized for public consumption. It needs a narrative to help it go down easier. To have raw data and files dumped out there is a nightmare." She put one of her mobiles down, freeing up a hand to reach for a scotch Gene poured her earlier. She winced as the liquid burned its way down her throat.

"Amateur," George whispered.

"The analytics on social and the web are showing threats of violence increasing every hour," she said.

"It'll calm down," George replied, waving her off.

"Did you see the fires started by protestors in Dallas?" said Gene, pointing toward the screen monitor on his wall. None of the channels being monitored had returned to normal programming since the news broke that morning.

"I just called my mother in Providence," Martea added. "Told her to lock her doors and stay inside until the protests calm down."

"And those are the newest ones," continued Gene. "San Diego, Alexandria, Pittsburg...Even the fucking hippies in Vermont are pissed off and taking to the streets."

"It'll pass," George whispered. He tried his best to keep from looking at the footage of protestors on the news.

"The whole God damn world was just told that everything they know about life is wrong," Martea yelled. "And worse yet, they also learned that we were considering not telling them, depending on what further study of the 'Seven Signal' revealed."

"Seven Signal?" Gene asked.

"That's what one of the anchors on public access called it this afternoon," Martea said, "Folks on social picked it up and ran with it."

"Well, I wish I was going to be here to help you with it," George said, reaching for the bottle of single malt on Gene's desk.

"Oh no! If we're going down, you're going with us, buddy!" Gene wagged his finger. He smiled for the first time in hours.

"Afraid not," George said as he poured himself a double.

"What do you mean?" Martea looked up from her apps that compiled social analytics in real-time.

"Well, I just gave POTUS my resignation, and she accepted it."

"You what?" Martea was dumbstruck.

"You can't be serious," Gene said, laughing in disbelief.

"Most of those emails were mine," George shrugged.

"Putting yourself on the sacrificial altar isn't going to calm the situation down," Martea said. "This is not some minor scandal where one head will do the trick! This is a full-blown crisis unlike anything we have ever seen! Not just here, but across the whole freaking planet."

George let out a long, defeated breath. "I'm old, Mar. I'm almost seventy-five. Neither of you would have ever emailed things like that so carelessly. The content of the emails was bad enough, but the stuff I attached to them was even worse. The sound files that we thought might have been music, the images…"

"Personally, I can't believe Candace is going to let you leave that easily," Gene chuckled. "I heard someone say they saw steam coming out of her ears two hours ago."

"I think she realizes this is bigger than we can understand right now," Martea said.

"What do you mean?" Gene's head tilted with curiosity.

"She's on a call with a dozen world leaders right now," Martea said. "Jean just sent me the pictures for her social channels."

"Yeah, I saw the memo about the call being scheduled. POTUS, the Vice President, and a few members of the Joint Chiefs. She was tight-lipped about it," Gene said.

George looked out the window. At the end of the lawn behind the fence, he could see a swarm of people. Some were holding up angry signs. Some were praying. Others were holding microphones. He could not tell which were press and which were podcasters trying to get their downloads up.

"I think she will be able to handle it," George said at last. He reached up to rub his eyes.

Gene looked at him. "Do you know what the meeting is about?"

Martea put down her mobiles and leaned forward. George returned to staring out the window at the crowd surrounding the White House. She reached out and touched his arm.

"George?"

George gave a weak smile. "Yeah, sorry! I'm just tired." He patted her hand before looking back at Gene. "POTUS is talking with the leaders of a dozen countries. I believe she's going to try to make the case that we should work together on the signal."

"Which means what?" Martea made another attempt to sip her drink.

"We've had this thing for months and don't know anything about it. I think Park has realized the resources of four countries may not be enough to analyze whatever the hell it is. It's organized, yes, but we can't identify or decipher what any of the information is. We can't even begin to speculate what the sounds are. We don't have a clear indication what the digital images represent. Is it someone's version of the Golden Record? Is it a warning? Was it meant for someone else, and we just found it by accident? Our best minds have no idea."

"So, what is she going to do?" Gene asked.

"The president is going to invite world leaders and their scientific teams to a summit. She's going to propose an open forum where information can be exchanged, and the best minds can work on finding out more about whatever the fuck this thing is." George poured himself another drink before removing his glasses and slipping them into his coat pocket.

"Why?" Gene asked.

"I think your speech inspired her, my friend," laughed George. "You wrote that line about being more transparent and doing it in broad view of the public. She's taking that as gospel."

"The president doesn't have time for summits and conferences." Martea waved her hands in the air. "She's got an election in ten months and campaign stops to make. Primaries are all around us!"

George paused, looking into his glass again before turning his eyes to Martea. "She feels this is more important."

"How can it be more important than her reelection? She won't be able to deal with it if she's out of office next year."

"Because if she does not get everyone onboard, now, with total transparency and cooperation, she feels the damage may never be undone. Trust was broken on so many levels, especially with our allies and partners."

"And the public." Martea looked back down at her analytics.

***

President Candace Park sat at her desk. With the cameras off and the meeting with a dozen world leaders over, she allowed herself to slump back into her chair. She reached over and tapped the intercom after a few long minutes ticked by.

"Send George in, please."

She stood up and walked over to one of the windows towards the rear of the Oval Office, shaking her head at the number of people outside the fence. Her gaze did not waver as George walked in.

"Madam President?" he asked.

"Take a seat, George."

"Okay." He waddled over and sat down on one of the couches across from the desk. "How did it go?"

"That's a question for a Chief of Staff," she replied.

"Yes, ma'am."

"I need to talk to my friend who has been with me since my first congressional race. Not a Chief of Staff."

"Yes, ma'am."

"Oh, give me a fucking break, George," Candace said, sitting down behind the Resolute Desk. She let out a long breath before glancing at the picture of her husband and daughter on a nearby table. "Am I doing the right thing?"

"Yes, Candace, I believe you are," he said.

"It feels like the world's ending," Candace said, motioning back to the window.

"I've left you with a hell of a mess. I'm so, so sorry…"

"Forget about that, okay? Just tell me what you think."

George shrugged his shoulders. "You're really going to pull out of the race? Forgo the election? I mean, a few small leaks before this one cannot undo the good you've achieved. Bipartisan bills, a good economy, and the London Accords are just some of accomplishments you can tout."

Candace threw her hands up. "I don't have time to worry about an election! I would rather use the next year to do something, anything, to fix this." She walked closer to the window to look at the protestors beyond the fence. "I don't want to be remembered as the president who gave people an excuse to torch the world and then threw out the fire extinguisher."

"I wish I could help you," George sighed. "But I'm more toxic than a bath at Yucca Mountain."

"I wish you could be there, too, my friend." Candace stood up and walked over to her phone. "Let's just hope the meeting goes well."

"You'll do fine," George said with a smile.

2039

"Jerome, get in here, please!"

The junior linguist closed his eyes and sighed. He was only three hours into what would probably be a twelve-hour shift. While he was delighted to have qualified for Project Seven, there were times he wished he was back at MIT gearing up to defend his dissertation. He had been recruited two years ago by the Department of Defense while still a fresh doctoral candidate. After a year of the best and brightest hitting walls, governments across the world decided to start looking for experts outside their employ.

Jerome Goldmann pushed his chair back, grabbed his tablet, and forced himself out into the hallway and towards Colonel Russell's office. He paused before walking in long enough to close his eyes and take a deep breath.

"Jerome, good! Come in. Sit down," Russell said, gesturing to the seat in front of him. "I wanted an update for the president."

"The president?" Jerome asked as he sat down. He could not tell if he was shifting in his seat because the chair was uncomfortable, or because the Colonel's voice was so grating.

"Yes, the president. He's going to be meeting soon with a dozen other world leaders on a call and wants to know if our team has made any discernable progress." Colonel Russell sat back in his seat. He twirled a pen with his fingers.

"Well, C-Colonel Russell," Jerome stammered, "we send you daily progress reports. So far, there has been nothing of note since—"

"Since you found repeating sets of characters within the text images from the Signal. Yes, I know. I also know that you are the one who found it while working with those two boys from China and that girl from Ireland. But that was three months ago. President Weir does not have the kind of patience you might assume from watching him on TV, and mine is wearing thin."

"Colonel, I want to give you answers. I really do. But it is a miracle that we've found anything so far. And honestly, it was by accident. There were thousands of pages of content in the Seven Signal." Jerome paused to take a sip from his water bottle. Being in Colonel Russell's office always made his mouth dry.

"It is not just a matter of decoding the words as if they would easily transcribe to English. The symbols, the way they seem to be organized, the structure is complete foreign to us. It is unlike any human language past or present." Jerome gestured with his hands as he spoke. "There is repetition, but what it means, we still don't know."

"Yes, yes, I know all that," Russell snapped, waving his hand in the air. "I'll be honest with you. When a twenty-four-year-old made the first real sign of progress in three years, it got everyone's attention. Now I'm beginning to wonder if you just got lucky."

Jerome clenched his jaw.

"There are a lot of other bright kids who would like a chance at your job, Jerome. Show me something else or make way for someone who can."

"Yes, Colonel," Jerome whispered.

"That's all, Jerome." The Colonel turned his attention to the tablets on his desk. Jerome stood up as silently as he could and slinked out the door.

As he made the short walk back to his area, he found himself wishing he could put in a call to his father, who had been an AI developer up until a few years ago when production on such engines was severely restricted, if not outright banned.

While initially conceived as a tool to ease the burdens of everyday life, the reveal of the Seven Signal showed just how much damage AI programming could do in the wrong hands. A decade of deepfakes, misinformation, and fraud gave rise to an exhausted public and frustrated government officials who found it impossible to deliver a cohesive narrative about work on Project Seven.

Worse yet, the leaders of many private corporations faced little consequence as their software was misused, turning a blind eye in exchange for the metadata they acquired.

His father ended up leaving one of the larger companies in the United States shortly before over one hundred countries signed the Bern Treaty on Artificial Intelligence. He shook his head, wishing he could get one of those self-directing algorithms to look at Project Seven's notes.

A minute later he was back at his desk, wiping the sweat from his brow.

"How was it?"

Jerome turned to look at Hylen Laurent, a recently minted Ph.D. from Cambridge who was visiting for a few weeks as part of Project Seven's exchange program. It was an idea from former President Candace Park during the last few months of her presidency.

While half the civilized world seemed to be in constant abject panic, President Park worked tirelessly to sow the seeds of something new within the international community. Whether she was driven purely by guilt or a sense of duty, she was determined to repair some of the damage done by the leak.

She went above and beyond, taking the time to organize the structure of it herself. She logged endless hours on Air Force One, hopping from one head of state to another, meeting with top officials, and volunteering several facilities within the United States as headquarters for what would become Project Seven. Its mission was to unlock the secrets of the signal.

President Park kept focus as her poll numbers sank. She continued meeting with world leaders, scientists, and military leaders despite the cries from her party who believed bowing out of the election to be a mistake. The Bern Treaty was signed a week before her assassination, eight months after leaving office.

Half the world was still afraid. The other seemed to always be looking for ways to burn it down. But Project Seven was now officially off the ground, with plenty of round-the-clock security.

"Jerome?" Hylen signed his name as she spoke. Having never been formally trained in sign language, Jerome had tried his best to pick up a few basic words and phrases as the days passed. The last thing he wanted to do was come off like Colonel Russell, who just yelled at her.

Jerome shook himself out of his daze. He faced her so she could read his lips better. "Sorry, Hylen," he said, moving his fist around his chest in a circle. "That was just the last thing I needed right now."

"Did he threaten to send you packing?" Hylen continued to sign as they talked.

"Yeah, how did you know?"

"He did the same to me before I went on my lunch break."

Jerome blinked. "But you've barely gotten started here!"

Hylen laughed. "I don't think that matters to him."

"Results should matter to him. And he should know that results take time," Jerome hissed. He thumped his fingers against his keyboard, waking his terminal from its rest. "You've been working with the audio files from the signal more than anyone else."

"Those things have vocal cords like a cello. I've never worked with sounds like this before. So smooth." Her hand moved from an "O" to an "A" sign in a soft, sweeping motion to emphasize the smoothness, humming the syllables.

Jerome found it remarkable how someone born without hearing could make a career out of analyzing sound waves. The only deaf people he had met before coming to work at Project Seven utilized implants to minimize their impairment, but Hylen declined to do so. Her terminal was outfitted with a special panel that she could place her palm on that translated sounds into tiny vibrations. Between that and the algorithm converting the files to digital waves on her screen, she had no trouble working with the rest of the team.

"Well, if they even have vocal cords," Jerome mused.

"The point is, I get it. The pressure on him must be enormous," Hylen said, signing as she spoke. "For him to start ratcheting up the demands on his team so suddenly."

"Pressure on him?" Jerome struggled not to laugh.

"I know our jobs our tough, but have you watched any newsreels recently?" Hylen swiveled in her chair to look at him.

"Not recently, why?" Jerome said.

Hylen shook her head and picked up her mobile. She pressed the icon for Teller, one of the larger social media networks. She scrolled through several images and videos of worldwide protests. Jerome watched in silence.

It never failed to amaze him how dedicated some people could be at taking the most important scientific discovery of all time and twisting it into something horrible. Some got creative and found ways to make money off fear and panic. Others cloaked themselves in faith and preached anger. Terrorism around the world continued to rise.

Jerome admitted to himself that he may not have wanted to watch the news because he feared a reminder of how shaky things were. Many in the scientific community assumed that as more information came to light, people would stop worrying and unify around just what an amazing thing it was. We were not alone. Something had reached out.

But for that to happen, people like Colonel Russell needed to know what to tell people. And all linguists, physicists, and eggheads like Jerome could give him was a list of some repeating symbols with no apparent meaning.

Jerome sighed and turned back to his computer.

***

Jerome rubbed his eyes as he struggled against the exhaustion weighing him down. Together with Hylen, he had sifted through pages of alien data for nearly two days. Opting to sleep on a cot near his desk, he only left the compound to go home and make sure his cat still had food and water in his bowls.

"Wait. Go back," Hylen said over her shoulder. Their monitors were linked, allowing the sharing of information instantaneously.

"Did you see something?" Jerome turned his head so she could see his lips move.

"Yes, go back."

Jerome flipped a few pages back until he felt a frenzied hand reach back and touch his shoulder.

"Right there, Jerome. Right there!"

"What is it? I don't see anything." He stared blankly at the screen.

"Hold on," she said before swiveling her chair around and reaching for her terminal. She turned up the volume knob on her display, which was usually kept low because she relied on visual and tactile interfaces. "Listen."

Jerome smiled as he listened to the deep, graceful tone of the notes. "I'd almost forgotten how beautiful it sounds."

Hylen said nothing, instead moving her sound file back to the beginning. "Go back to the very first page of symbols!" She looked to make sure he was on page one before continuing. "Follow along with your eyes."

Hylen pressed play and turned to watch Jerome's display. A smile slowly crossed her face as she pointed to the symbols along with the sound of the notes. Jerome turned to see her one hand was still on her touch pad, feeding her vibrations as the sounds went.

Jerome listened as a long swell of sound pitched up, bending in a way unlike anything that was possible on any stringed instrument he had ever heard. He thought back to how he used to listen to his father practice guitar years ago. With the use of pitch-shifting pedals, he could make a low E jump up two or more octaves in the most fun and unnatural ways.

"Can you start it over again!" said Jerome, looking at Hylen. She nodded, waiting for him to go back to the first page of symbols once again.

Whereas music notes on staff paper moved from left to right in rows, the notes on these pages seemed to flow out from the top, moving in a graceful counterclockwise motion towards the center of the page. As he flipped to the next page, he discovered the sequence would start from the center of and go clockwise out to the edge. The patterns continued page after page.

"Why did they have to make this so damned hard?" Jerome said to her.

"To them, this could be child's play," Hylen smiled. "Or maybe it's a test. They might not want anyone to respond if they didn't have the time and attention span to figure it out. But I think we have something here, you and I."

"It's like sheet music. So, what? They reached out to us in song? Are we dealing with an entire planet of Broadway singers?"

"It may not be singing," Hylen said. "This may be how they communicate. Maybe song to them is like speech to us. Or maybe it's completely different for written and verbal communication." She looked back to her vibration pad. "But it is beautiful!"

Before Jerome could speak, she reached over to the comms panel on her desk.

"Colonel, could you please come to station A-5? We have something here we would like you to see."

"Oh, shit," Jerome groaned before straightening up in his chair. The Colonel strode up to their section, still wearing his sunglasses.

"What do you two have?" Russell asked.

"Listen," Hylen said, putting her finger to her lips. "Jerome, show him on your monitor. Page one."
Hylen moved her chair aside and pressed play on her recording. She turned up the volume louder. Russell leaned over as others in the office began to gather around their station.

"And what exactly is this?"

"This, Colonel, may just be a sentence. Or a paragraph." Hylen's smile was broader than Jerome had ever seen it.

"What do you mean? Is it something, or isn't it?"

"We still don't know what it says. But it is the first real sign of progress in months. The sound files follow along with whatever these symbols and notations say on the digital pages."

"And this can't be coincidence?"

"No, I don't believe so," Hylen said.

"I don't think so either," Jerome added. "The characters follow along. They're longer when the notes on the recording are held. They grow bolder as the sounds get louder. And the pattern they seem to follow from page to page is too specific to be random."

Russell leaned in closer. "Have you sent this to anyone else yet?"

"No," Jerome said. "We wanted to show you first."

"Well, what the hell are you waiting for? Get whoever you need to help you make sense of this. I want a report on my desk with the next five hours." He straightened up and walked away.

"That's gratitude for you," Jerome breathed. Hylen laughed and prepared to transfer their newly composited image.

***

Three months had passed since their alien sheet music discovery went out to research teams in over a dozen countries. Was it music? Did they communicate entirely in song, or was it simply how their language sounded? The announcement stirred the imaginations of everyone in the program. One inspired linguist even sent around a doodle of a symphony being loaded onto a spaceship while the ambassadors, soldiers, and politicians were left behind.

After all this time, music was all Jerome could see. Hylen once commented how the sound waves reminded her of a cello. To him, the symbols on the page looked as if someone attempted to represent musical notes artistically. The meaning of it all was still elusive, but at least now there seemed to be a correct way to take it in.

Jerome straightened his necktie. He rarely wore them, mostly due to the fact they always ended up feeling horribly uncomfortable. In a few minutes, he would be called into an office with presidents, prime ministers, scientists, and high-ranking military personnel from over forty countries across the globe.

He heard footsteps coming up behind him, which he assumed belonged to Hylen. He failed to turn and look, still fiddling with the tie that was doing all it could not to cooperate. A deep, baritone voice startled him.

"I've not had the chance to offer my congratulations to you, Mr. Goldmann."

Jerome froze, instantly recognizing the voice. He turned slowly, hoping his face did not reveal too much embarrassment.

"Thank you, Mr. President."

"It's me who should be thanking you, young man. You and Miss Laurent," President Weir said. Tall, trim, and flashing a broad smile, Jerome always thought he looked like a caricature of a president. He extended his hand to Jerome.

"I'm just happy to help, Mr. President." Jerome said as he shook Weir's hand. "I wish our discovery had given us more of an indication as to what the message contained. I know things take time, but I want to know what it is they want. What they are trying to say."

"I have a hunch you and your partner Hylen unlocked more than you realize." Weir flashed another smile. "To see something in its proper context is often the first step to understanding it." He pivoted to face the door. "So, I've heard you'll be headed back to MIT soon?"

"Um, yes, Mr. President," said Jerome. "I'm looking forward to finishing my Ph.D."

"They should be rolling out a red carpet for you two, after what you've accomplished." He held up his hand for a second, anticipating another hollow expression of thanks. "Did you know that yesterday was the first day without a death related to the signal in the United States in the past three years? Not one riot, mass shooting, or suicide claimed a life yesterday." Weir stood still for a moment, his expression growing more solemn. "In a minute I'm going to walk in there and introduce you and your partner as the wunderkinds who put us on the path toward understanding the Seven Signal someday soon. But right now, I don't give a damn about that. I just want to thank you for saving some lives."

Jerome stood still, unsure of what to say as President Weir continued.

"New things lead to fear. Fear leads to confusion. Confusion leads to panic when no rational answers are available. It's entirely predictable, yet still shocking every time we see it. Yesterday the world learned that we have made progress and now have a new understanding of how to look at a message sent from someone 300 light-years outside this solar system." Weir put his hand on Jerome's shoulder. "For years, everyone has been waiting to hear just the tiniest little bit of information. Thank you for giving us something to say."

Jerome wiped away a tear as he took it in. Hylen was right when she commented how he never kept up with the news. It was far easier to block it out and focus on his job when it seemed as if everyone he knew was met with constant agitation from strangers and distrust from loved ones. Hearing that their discovery may have even had a marginally positive impact hit him far deeper than he would have guessed.

President Weir opened the door and walked through, shaking hands with Colonel Russell on his way to the podium. Jerome followed, trying to straighten up as much as he could next to the towering politician. He did his best not to look at the cameras from news agencies around the world. A smile crossed his face as Hylen stood up from the table with representatives from the United Kingdom and came up next to him.

"Good morning," President Weir said with another practiced smile. "I'm delighted to be here today with two of the individuals responsible for this new breakthrough. Like many of you, I have waited for the past three years to learn what the Seven Signal contains. And as tempting as it is to keep talking in front of this much press, I'm going to shut up, step aside, and let our experts take it away."

Weir gestured for the two to step up to the mass of microphones in front of them before walking over to Martea Salazar, who was getting ready to take some pictures.

Hylen gave Jerome a wink and stepped up to the microphone. Unlike him, she had no fear of public speaking, which is why they agreed earlier that she should be the one to present the news. Her delivery would undoubtedly go over better than Jerome's propensity to stammer in front of a crowd.

"Good morning, everyone!" Hylen said, bringing her palm down from her chin and raising it from under her other arm. "We are both so excited to be here today to discuss our latest findings with the data from the Seven Signal." Hylen turned to Jerome with a glance that reminded him to smile. "I wanted to begin by addressing the elephant in the room: the strife created in the wake of the signals' discovery." She paused to take a note card out of her jacket pocket.

"It has been far too easy to focus on the conflict brought about by the news that we are not alone in the universe. What should have been the most joyous news in human history was met with anger, division, ugly politics, and fear. And with so much focus on those negative elements, we have lost focus on what we have gained as a people."

Jerome nodded along as his colleague continued to speak and sign.

"I am a member of the team here in Maryland that contains scientists and officials from over twenty countries. There are now dozens like it across the globe. We are all part of 'the exchange,' a nickname we in Project Seven gave ourselves. Working in cooperation and unity with fellow scientists and researchers in another part of the world has been the honor of my life."

She took a deep breath in before continuing. "Countries that are allies can use Project Seven to strengthen their bonds. Those who were once enemies can use it to forge new ones. While we have learned bits and pieces, I fear we will never grasp the full context of the message unless all of us work together."

Jerome looked over to President Weir, whose smile was far more genuine than the one he normally presented to the cameras.

"Today, thanks to the efforts of brilliant minds like Jerome Goldmann and others, we are beginning to understand the information contained in the signal." Hylen motioned to the monitor on her left. "The notations on these pages appear to go along with the sounds we have all heard over the past few years."

A hushed whisper took over the room. Hylen nodded for one of the techs off to the side to play a sample of the sound files over the video presentation. Highlighted notation on the page spiraled outwards in perfect synchronization as the musical voicings lifted and fell.

"Knowing how to arrange the data gives us the opportunity to examine everything contained within the Seven Signal. It is truly breathtaking when combined with newly uncovered digital images. Many of these have never been revealed to the public before now. Let's have a look!"

Hylen grinned as one of those new images took over the main monitor. It was surrounded by more of that musical script. Whether it was a name, a caption, or something else entirely was still unknown, but it was stunning for the group to look at.

A round of applause broke out in the room. Jerome found himself almost giddy with excitement.

"This," Hylen said, "is a shape found many times throughout the signal's data. We believe it may be a representation of what these aliens look like."

The form did not look anything like the aliens portrayed in movies or on streaming serials. It looked no larger than a gray wolf. It had four legs for walking and two other limbs tucked up against its chest toward the front. Each of those forward limbs appeared to have some sort of grasping appendage on the end. Above those was a head, maybe. And while it was more akin to a detailed line drawing than a photograph, it still drew impressed gasps from the crowd.

"This is a species intelligent enough to send out a signal whose inner workings baffled our brightest minds for years. Sixty-two years ago, humanity sent out the Voyager probes with a message of peace and friendship. There is every reason to believe this was their intention as well." Hylen tucked her notecard back into her pocket.

"Now that we know this, what will we do with it? We know this signal was sent out over three centuries ago, from a solar system so far away, and yet so very close.

Three hundred light years seems like an impossible distance, but as my friends in the physics department keep telling me, that is practically next door."

Jerome stiffened with the realization that Hylen was going off script.

"What will we do next?" she asked.

J.D. Sanderson

2104

Jaken Kolisnyk stared into the open door of the enormous hangar. He grew up reading about facilities like this, back when only countries like the United States and Russia were launching people into space. Those hangars were less than half the size of Home Base One, which measured nearly one million square feet.

Inside the enormous structure was a miniature metropolis filled with engineers, physicists, technicians, and administrative personnel. Jaken ran his hands over his thin beard before walking inside.

"Jaken! Glad you're here! Welcome to your new home." Director Kavya Reddy waved him over to a large computer terminal. She had a dozen individuals around her, all in dark blue tech uniforms.

"Thank you," Jaken said. He smiled as the director introduced him to the techs who were working on the new experiment at the heart of Home Base One.

"This way, Jaken," Kavya said, motioning with her hand to a flight of stairs leading to a second level of offices.

"Thank you." Jaken did his best to keep up with her while looking toward the center of the hangar. There were too many people, vehicles, and display screens in front of him to get a good look.

Words failed him as he reached the top of the stairs took in the experimental craft for the first time in person. The silvery sweeping primary hull housed enough room for a crew of ten. At the rear was a state-of-the-art gravity drive. The prototype fusion engine inside was powerful enough to light up half of his home city of Odessa.

"My God," Jaken gasped.

"She's beautiful, isn't she? They're calling her the crown jewel of The Exchange."

"Test flights next year?"

"Maybe sooner if we are lucky. Construction is still wrapping up, but we will have you in there soon enough." Kavya led Jaken down a shiny catwalk to another cluster of people. "This is most of our core administrative team here at Home Base. Charel is our Operations Director, Miller oversees medical, Moussa heads up life sciences, and this is Leandra, our head of public relations."

Leandra extended her hand. "It's nice to meet you, Captain Jaken."

"You as well," Jaken said. He smiled politely for a second before turning back around to the ship. "When can I go inside?"

"Later today. I'll have Leandra take you inside and get some photographs," Kavya said.

"Photographs?" Jaken tilted his head.

"Welcome to life in Home Base," Moussa said with a laugh. "The PR never ends, especially when it comes to our star test pilot! The press is going to love hearing all about the man who is going to take us across the solar system."

***

Jaken took a hover transport over to the crew barracks a half a kilometer away from the hangar. He snapped a picture with his wristcom, frowning when he realized the image inadvertently captured a few protestors at the end of the fencing.

The image brought back memories of his early years at school. As a child, it was alarming to learn how discovery of the Seven Signal led to years of tension across the globe. A group of isolationism extremists even managed to sabotage the first major Project Seven command center thirty years earlier. No lives were lost, but the damage from the improvised device crippled the buildings' structure, leading the world governments to further disseminate the project. Decentralization meant less risk over time.

For over sixty-five years, governments across the world were slowly coming together with a common goal: Learn more about the Seven Signal. At the beginning, public opinion was so low that Project Seven was almost abandoned. It was not until scientists finally figured out how to organize the signal data that the public began to come around.

Decades later, it was an accepted way of life. Each new scientific discovery made by Project Seven led to new breakthroughs in agriculture, medicine, and energy.

Private sector industries were also regularly working in tandem with governments. There was even talk of using limited AI functions to assist with some of the more challenging aspects of space exploration, but that would require an amendment to The Bern Treaty.

Globally, nearly seventy percent of people approved of the work The Exchange was doing. More than just the controlling agency of Project Seven, The Exchange was rapidly becoming the umbrella under which most of the world's governing bodies met and worked together.

Jaken picked up his bag from the back seat of the hover transport and thanked the driver. Removing his badge from his shirt, he held it up to a small round panel next to the doorway. The panel changed color and beeped when it finished confirming his identity, opening the door.

Instead of unpacking, Jaken took a moment to call home. His wife and daughter answered the call.

"Hi, Daddy!" His daughter beamed at the camera, smiling and waving. He waved back as his wife Wenda entered the frame.

"How is it?" Wenda asked. "Are you in the barracks?"

"Yeah, I'm here. This whole place is amazing. I can't wait for you to come and see it!"

"When will that be, Daddy?" asked his four-year-old daughter, Beki.

"Another few weeks, Beki. They are just starting to build the family lodging. They're printing the main structures soon, though. I'll send you pictures when they're up. I already have our plot picked out, right next to where the playground is going to be!"

"I can't wait," Wenda said. "My boss keeps asking when I will be making the switch to my new home office." She giggled as Beki pushed her face back in front of the camera, taking up the entire frame.

"Daddy! Daddy! Did you see the ship?"

"I did, Beki! It is *so* big!" Jaken replied, holding out his hands.

"Is it bigger than your room?"

"Oh yeah, way bigger than my room."

"Want to see a picture I drew for you?" Beki smiled up to the camera.

"Oh, she worked hard on this one," Wenda said, stroking her daughter's hair. "She made it in art class and couldn't wait to show you on tonight's call."

"Let me see it," Jaken said with a smile. He watched as his daughter held up a picture showing a stick figure astronaut and a blue, red, and green drawing of the prototype ship.

"It's beautiful! You drew that all by yourself?"

Beki nodded as she pointed out all the different parts of the ship she learned about in school. "Do you want to put it up in your office?" she asked.

"Of course, I do!" Jaken laughed. "You could grow up to be an artist like your mother!"

"I want to be a scientist, daddy!" Beki smiled.

The call went on for another twenty minutes before Jaken decided he was in desperate need of something to eat. He waved goodbye to his family and walked into what he guessed was supposed to be kitchen.

"Okay, what do we have here?" He wondered aloud. Inside the fridge showed a stack of ready-to-eat meals for all times of the day. While he did not mind eating vegetarian, he was happy to see there were still some humane meat options available. He took one out and put it into the heating drawer.

***

Jaken settled into a new routine over the next several days, familiarizing himself with the ship, learning more about the inner workings of Home Base One, and getting to know several of his Project Seven counterparts. After a very long shift, he would hop onto the transport and reflect on his day, often using the brisk few minutes to look back at his notes.

Each day he passed the same group of protestors outside the fence. There were never more than ten of them, holding signs in silence.

At the end of the fifth day, he was informed by the transport operator that one of the thrusters needed repairs.

"Sorry, Mr. Kolisnyk. This damn thing hasn't been working for two hours. I'm almost done if you don't mind waiting another twenty or thirty minutes?"

"That's okay Karol, I don't mind the walk. It's not too far and the weather is nice." Jaken shifted his tablets in his arms and walked out the side entrance of the hangar. He walked along the fence, taking in the vast prairie landscape off in the distance.

Fifteen minutes later he found himself walking past the group of protestors. One of them standing at the end, several steps from the others, looked up and nodded. His sign warned about stopping the 'Century Movement,' a popular conspiracy theory about how Project Seven was actually a front for an elaborate takeover by elites.

"Hello," Jaken said politely.

"Hello," the young man replied.

Jaken walked by before turning around to look at the quiet protestor again. "What exactly are you trying to do here?"

"Pardon?" The young man lowered his sign below his head.

"I asked why you're here," Jaken said. He looked back to the massive hangar. "Why does this bother you so much?"

"Why doesn't it bother you?"

"Oh, it does sometimes. Keeps me too busy. Makes me work too hard. But it's amazing to think about what we're going to be doing soon." Jaken looked up at the sky. "It's worth it to me."

"You really believe there are aliens out there?"

"I do," Jaken said.

"Why?"

"Because every verifiable scientific method on the planet has confirmed the Seven Signal is real. We've all worked together to try and learn more for two generations."

"And for two generations, we've all been slowly amassing under one single regime."

Jaken studied the protestor. He did not look disheveled or confused, and he spoke like he had a decent amount of education. There was no immediate indication he was a stimulant or downer junkie. Some of the others that stood out there day after day had the unmistakable look of someone who had not gotten out of the house enough. This guy was different.

"The Exchange has been growing, yes," Jaken said. "It's a partnership. A level of cooperation we have never seen before. But that does not mean there is anything subversive about it."

The young man smiled again. "You seem cool, man. I hope you get out of here soon."

Unsure what to say next, Jaken smiled, nodded, and proceeded on his walk back to the barracks.

***

Two days later Jaken decided to walk back to his room. After spending most of the day sitting still in a simulator and was desperate for a chance to stretch his legs. The young protestor from the other day smiled and waved to him.

"Hey there, friend. You decided to give up working for the tyrants yet?"

Jaken laughed. "I don't think so. I'm pretty happy with my gig."

"What do they have you doing there, might I ask?"

Jaken hesitated, remembering countless briefings about protestors and conspiracy theorists. Despite all those warnings, there was very little about this person that set off any red flags. He decided then there was no harm in talking, as long as he proceeded with an appropriate level of caution.

"I'm betting you know I'm not supposed to give away any details. We have regular interviews and press releases for a reason." Jaken said.

"Yeah, it's okay. I've seen that insider post your picture on the Project Seven PR pages," the man said.

"Insider?" Jaken asked. He remained determined not to take the bait and give away too much.

"Yeah, the multi-generational you have in there. She's proof it's part of a family of people who run everything, man. Don't you know?"

"I'm sorry, but you seem to have more knowledge than me in this case," Jaken said, trying not to giggle at the sound of it all.

"Leandra," the man said, before turning and holding up his sign. Jaken froze momentarily before turning to head home once more.

***

"He said what?"

"Pretty weird, isn't it?" Jaken said. "Can you pass me the vinegar?"

"Weirdest shit I've heard in a long time," Moussa said before handing a small bottle to Jaken. "Did you tell Leandra yet? I bet she'd get a kick out of it."

"No, I don't want to make her feel weird. I mean, I get it, she is in the public eye. She deals with that stuff all day every day. It figures they would know who she is." Jaken looked down at his meal, stirring it with his fork.

"She will not care." Moussa looked over to the queue and waved at Leandra. "Hey! Come here!"

"No, hey. Come on. I don't want her to think I'm talking about her to some conspiracy theorist whacko." Jaken tried to object further, but Leandra was already sitting down.

"What's going on?" she asked.

"Nothing," Jaken said, "just some crazies out along the fence again."

"One of them was talking about you, my friend!" Moussa smiled, toasting her with his water. "Apparently you are part of a generational conspiracy."

"Oh, that," Leandra laughed, popping open her water. "It's been a while since I've been called a multi-gen."

"You've heard that before?" Jaken asked her.

"Well, it's not some big secret. My grandmother Martea worked in the White House for President Park when the signal was received. She later worked for the next administration under President Weir in a different role.

"So public life is kind of a family business then, I take it?"

"Well, my mother stayed out of public life entirely. I've always loved taking pictures, and I grew up admiring my grandmother so much. I figured I might as well post them on social for the government," Leandra said. "Over time, it evolved into my position as head of public relations here at Home Base. It was either that or put my degree in digital media to use in the jungle, and big animals scare me. Anyway, I wouldn't listen to those guys out there."

Jaken shrugged. "They seem harmless enough. Just read too much shit online."

"There's harmless, and then there's harmless," Leandra said. "They may not be planting bombs anymore, but they still work to spread false information."

"Nothing a few actual friends wouldn't cure," Moussa said.

***

The family housing units would be complete in another week. Jaken held up his wristcom to take a picture for Beki, who asked him about what they looked like every chance she got. He clicked a button and sent it off to Wenda. A reply of three hearts drew a smile across his face.

Jaken saw the young man again, this time with a smaller sign showing world leaders in alien hats.

"Pretty creative, my friend" Jaken laughed.

"Thank you," he said. "I'm Olin, by the way."

"Jaken."

"I know who you are," Olin said. "All over social, remember?"

"Oh yeah. I don't check it much," Jaken said. His job kept him busy enough during the day and tired enough at night to not care about browsing his social accounts.

"Probably healthier for you," Olin acknowledged with a nod.

Jaken looked up at the sky. The days were growing shorter, and a few stars were finally starting to appear as the sun moved closer to the horizon. "You don't seem like your fellow anarchists here. I'm curious. Why are you out here?"

"I just don't believe what they tell me. It's the same every day on the newsfeeds. Humanity is inspired. Humanity is together. Humanity is going to reach the stars." Olin let out a deep, tense breath. "We're going to meet other intelligent beings like us."

"I think we might," Jaken said.

"You really do?"

"Do I know for certain? No. The scientist in me must acknowledge there is a high probability we will never find anyone. We may not be capable of making it past the heliopause. But the pilot in me?" Jaken pointed to his heart. "That is the part that is hopeful. I mean, how can we not try?"

"Don't you think we should fix our own planet, first?"

"Well, forgive me for saying so, but we have done a pretty good job of that over the past few decades. Have you ever seen anyone go hungry? Can you remember the last global pandemic? I can't." Jaken took a step closer to the fence. "How many kids can read before entering kindergarten compared to those a hundred years ago?

"Just because there aren't any problems doesn't mean there aren't any problems," Olin said, pointing to the popular catchphrase on his shirt.

Shaking his head, Jaken said, "I think some people just need to complain about. Having to trust in things without fully understanding them can be a big leap."

"Why do you think that?" Olin asked.

"I don't know. Maybe some people just need to fight. Something to rally against." He lifted his arms up. "I was never like that, so I guess I can't understand. But I can empathize."

Olin said nothing, opting instead to stare down at his sign.

"I think that the idea of life beyond this little world is just too scary for some to think about," Jaken continued. "It makes people feel small, like looking at the Milky Way on a clear night. Only now, we know someone might be looking back. I see that and I don't feel fear. I feel hope!"

"Hope?"

"Yeah, hope. Have you ever read about the twentieth or early twenty-first century? You should if you haven't. It was quite the shitshow. People used to ponder how we would blow ourselves up. There even used to be a thing called a Doomsday Clock."

"Oh c'mon. Even I'm not going to believe that!"

"It's true. They used to move the minute hand closer and closer to midnight, predicting the end of the world." Jaken smiled. "And the end of the world might've come if we had not learned someone else was out there, waiting for us."

Jaken pointed to the wings next to his Exchange badge. "That's why I learned how to fly and developed a passion for science. I studied my whole life with the hope I could see what is out there."

"But the signal was just a bunch of dashes, weird drawings…"

"Until we learned how to arrange it. Everything is nonsense until you know what you're doing," Jaken smiled. "Words are just jumbled letters until they're put into the right order. Sixty-five years later, we are beginning to understand information about another world; a culture that thinks and feels. And that is wonderful."

Olin turned away from Jaken, closing his eyes.

"What's wrong?" Jaken asked.

"Nothing," the younger man said. "I have to go." He folded up his sign, nodded to one of the other protestors, and walked over to a small car in the parking lot. Jaken estimated it had to be over a hundred years old. Most cars that were still on the road had electric conversion kits installed since the world was increasingly less dependent on petroleum.

***

"Director Reddy? I have the President of India as requested."

"Thank you, Colee. Patch him in." Kavya wheeled her chair over to the monitor on her desk.

"Is that Director Reddy I see before me?" The elderly Indian leader adjusted his glasses as the communication feed came into focus.

"Mr. President! Thank you very much for taking the time to speak with me!" Kavya said. "I know you're busy, so I won't waste too much of your time."

"It is never a bad time for you, dear. What can I do for you?"

"I spoke with a few of our friends at The Exchange, and we're looking to expand our team here at Home Base One. I wanted to know if you had anyone in mind to join us. Or, perhaps, you could let others know we are looking." Kavya picked up a tablet. "I'm sending you a list of open positions here."

"Thank you for letting me know. I'm sure we can come up with something." The president looked down at the data as it loaded on his display.

A knock on Kavya's door interrupted their conversation. "Can you excuse me one second, Mr. President?" She reached over and muted the channel on her way over to the door. Jaken was waiting for her on the other side.

"Jaken, I thought you had gone back to your barrack hours ago. Is everything all right?

"I'm fine, yes. Thank you. I just need to speak with you about something if you have a minute," he said.

Kavya looked him over before letting him in. "Take a seat. One moment please." She reached and unmuted the channel. "Mr. President, I am sorry. I need to attend to something here. May we continue this conversation at another time?"

"Of course, dear," he said, closing the channel.

Kavya collected her tablets and stacked them in a tray on the corner of her desk. She regarded Jaken. While he lacked the joviality of most military pilots she knew, he was as calm and cool as anyone under her command. This evening, however, he looked almost nervous.

"What did you want to talk about?" Kavya asked.

"I realize this is going to sound silly, but I think I may have a security concern," Jaken replied. His fingers drummed on the armrest of his chair.

"The security of this facility and the ability to continue its work is of paramount importance," Kavya said. "Please continue."

"A few times this week, I had a discussion with one of the protestors at the end of the fence. I realize it sounds silly. He engaged me when I had to walk home one day, one of the younger ones. Seemed harmless enough..."

"I've seen them out there every day for years," Kavya said. "Go on."

"This man, he is usually very pleasant. But today when he left, it seemed different. Something was off. I don't really know if I can describe it, but it was just a feeling."

"Do you know his name?"

"Olin. He said his name was Olin."

"Okay," Kavya said, turning to another panel on her desk. She tapped a command, which illuminated a screen on the wall next to her desk. A woman with dark skin, severe features, and gray hair appeared.

"Yes, Director Reddy?"

"Good evening, Secretary Akhtar. I'd like to request a security screening probe."

"Do you believe Home Base One is under threat?" asked Secretary Akhtar.

"We're not sure, but better safe than sorry. His first name is Olin, and he has been here recently with a small group of protestors."

"I will need to consult with the judiciary circle of The Exchange and obtain a warrant for the probe," Akhtar replied. "I'll let you know if it's granted."

"Thank you, Secretary," Kavya said before closing the channel. She turned back to Jaken. "They're usually pretty fast with this sort of thing."

"They need to get a warrant?" Jaken asked.

"Of course. The Exchange cannot peer into people's private lives without a warrant. Public-facing social accounts are fair game, but anything private needs a judge's signature."

Jaken sat back in his seat and ran his hands through his hair. "I'm sorry if this all ends up to be nothing."

"I never want people to apologize for caring about the project or the people who work here," she said. "Our job is to grow and learn, and we cannot do that if we feel we are under threat."

"I know there hasn't been any kind of attack on a Project Seven facility in years–"

"There hasn't been, no," Kavya interrupted. "But I understand. You and I are fortunate enough to live here, now, when most of the world is on board with our mission. But we all grew up reading history, and know what happened in London, Cairo, and Perth. People do terrible things when they act out of fear, and it would not take much to send ripples of it through society again."

***

Jaken sat back in the commander's seat of the test ship, running tests and simulations. The completed engine was set to be installed in a week's time, and he was excited to take it out of the hangar when the time came.

Through the main viewing portal, he could see the newly-completed family housing units. He smiled, imagining Beki and Wenda playing in their new backyard.

"Take a break, Jaken. Boss wants to see you!" Moussa called in on the headset. Jaken gave a thumbs up to the camera and left the command deck of the ship.

After a successful test of the ship's engines would come flights in the atmosphere. Low earth orbit would soon follow, along with a quick trip around the moon and back. And this was far from the only component of Project Seven. The Linguistics Division continued to analyze the Seven Signal, while Stellar Mapping continued to scan the skies for other signals.

There was always talk of one day getting beyond the confines of the Sol System and meeting the Signalers face-to-face. While linguistics was still unable to translate an exact name for their species, the nickname Signalers had stuck for quite a few years.

Jaken walked around the corner to see Leandra talking with Kavya. They waved him over.

"There you are, Captain," Kavya said, "I wanted to let you know we finally heard about your query from a few weeks back."

"I've been wondering about that. I haven't seen him by the fence in a while." Jaken gestured to the side door of the hangar. "I figured since you never got back to me with anything regarding the probe that nothing came of it. Did something happen?"

"Well, yes," Kavya began.

"I hope he's okay," Jaken said, looking off into the distance.

"He applied to college," Leandra said. She smiled over to Kavya, who seemed to find the confused look on Jaken's face amusing.

"College?" Jaken asked.

"That's right. He posted a video on his social channel today. He mentioned our facility, which is why it came up in my search. I've showed it to a few of my colleagues here, and I thought you'd like to see it as well."

Leandra handed him the tablet and excused herself. Jaken took a seat in one of the office chairs and pressed the playback button.

He watched the young man, whose full name was Olin McDowell, in a video titled *Why Not?*

"So, a few weeks ago I started talking to this guy who works at the Home Base Facility here in my hometown. You know the one, right? It's the huge building that blocks the entire sunset! Anyway, I was there as a protester. I had been against this stuff my entire life. I read all the pages and platforms online about how the government was slowly but surely executing its hundred-year plan."

Olin turned the camera around to show a computer screen. "So, after talking with this science guy, I decided to look up some of the things he told me. It blew my mind, people, let me tell you." The younger man wiped away a tear as he talked. "After a few days, I realized maybe what I thought was the truth, wasn't the whole truth. Or maybe it wasn't the truth at all."

Jaken listened intently as the young man discussed his plans to go to college in a few months. He had been accepted to a small institution in Minnesota and was interested in learning more about science and history. Olin concluded the video by thanking the 'science guy' at Home Base One.

Jaken smiled as he closed out the video.

J.D. Sanderson

2192

"*Abeona*, are you reading us?"

"This is the crew of the *Abeona*. We are receiving you Home Base One." Captain Dai Tanaka looked ahead as the bright surface of the moon swept across the main viewer and out of view. "Final check. Go."

"Medical monitoring looks good," Doctor Tallum Gladwell replied.

"Communications are green," Chief Moneca Chen said.

"Power levels are good. Heat and particle deflection system is good," Lieutenant Callum O'Shea added.

"Gravity drive is online and hot," Commander Walis Salah said. She patted the monitor in front of it. "And she is beautiful!" The command crew laughed.

Dai shook his head before touching the small circular pad on the side of his temple. "Home Base One, we are good to go and clear of Elpis Station in lunar orbit." The captain sipped his coffee as he sat up straight in his command chair. He could feel the gentle rotation of the ship's primary hull, which allowed for a fair approximation of Earth's gravity. The drive section in the rear was stationary and required the finesse of zero gravity training.

The mission director's voice came through again on the comm. "Acknowledged, *Abeona*. Are you ready, Dai?"

"I believe we all are, Home Base One." Dai smiled, entering coordinates into the *Abeona's* navigational system.

"Roger, *Abeona*. We have a special send-off for you. Please stand by."

The command crew looked around, unsure of what was coming their way from the control team back at Home Base One.

***

"Is it a bottle of champagne, by chance? If so, the time to open it was when we could all share it with you," Dai said. His voice echoed throughout the main control area at the top level of the Home Base One command complex.

"Not quite, Captain. This, I believe, will be even more special," Mission Director Derik Maali released the door seal, allowing a group of well-dressed men and women to enter. "We have The Exchange command council here in person to see you off!"

"Oh! You pulled the bureaucrats out of Bern, huh?" Dai asked. The sound of laughter from the crew of the *Abeona* filled the command deck as the lead council member walked up to the microphone with a smile on her face.

"Captain Tanaka, this is Councilor Altman. How is the view up there? Can you see my brother in the Kolisnyk Dome?"

"I knew there was someone I forgot to wave to," Dai said.

"Well, maybe you can catch him next time," Altman said. "We're here to tell you how incredibly proud we are of you. What you and your team are doing was the stuff of stories generations ago. But today, a crewed mission to swing by Uranus and Neptune! It is an amazing thing. I doubt even the founders of The Exchange ever believed we would make it this far."

"We're just happy to represent our people back home," Dai replied.

Altman smiled back at Maali, who gestured to several of the monitors on the wall. Rotating images of crowds watching from around the world filled the screens. Children held up signs with hand-drawn sketches of the *Abeona* as proud parents looked on.

"Over one hundred and fifty years ago, a young scientist working on Project Seven, asked a question during a press conference. She wondered what we would do next after learning that life existed elsewhere in the universe," Altman continued. "Her name was Hylen Laurent. Many of you will recognize that name as one of the first individuals elected to office on the promise of growing The Exchange into what it is today." She took a breath in. It was common for her to make speeches, but she had never done so with an estimated seventy-five percent of the planet watching.

"It was not easy for people then. They were worried, and scared, but they kept going. Now we have new technologies that allowed us to tackle problems that used to plague so many here on Earth. We expanded our presence to the moon, Mars, the asteroid belt, and Ganymede. Your mission today is the next step, and we are all very proud of you. Like many of you, I often wonder if the Signalers are still out there, watching over us. If so, I believe they would be impressed by what you are going to show us today."

Altman paused. She looked past the reporters to her fellow council members, Director Derik Maali, and the control technicians. Each had the blue, silver, and white emblem of The Exchange on their shoulder. For the first time in years, it was really sinking in just how far they had come.

"Good luck, *Abeona*. Godspeed."

***

Dai, Tallum, Moneca, Callum, and Walis exchanged glances as they listened to Altman's remarks. Dai opened the channel, allowing the ten crew members in the engine and storage areas to listen as well.

"Thank you, Councilor Altman. It means more than you know to us that people are watching from down below."

"I'm going to miss that little blue marble," Moneca whispered. She reached up and touched a picture of her three children that she stuck to the top of her station. "And all the people on it."

"Home Base One, this is the *Abeona*. With your permission, we would like to begin the countdown to activate the gravity drive."

"*Abeona*, you have a go," Director Waali said. "Make us proud!"

Dai nodded before looking over his shoulder. "Coordinates for burst one are programmed. How are we doing, Walis?"

"We're ready," Walis said. "This beauty is going to take us there almost twice the speed of those Inner System Drives."

"How is Archie doing?"

Walis looked over to a secondary panel that showed Archie, the imbedded AI algorithm that served as a backup on ship functions and calculations. Dai had chosen to name it Archie, after his favorite mathematician, Archimedes.

"Archie concurs," Walis said.

"Just be sure to give me a smooth ride, okay?" Tallum said. "I'm looking forward to dinner in a little while below deck."

"Beginning ten-second countdown," Dai announced.

***

The surrounding light from stars and planets dissolved and reformed into a soft, bright glow. To those on the command deck, it seemed to have no real beginning and no real end.

For most of his time in space, Dai had served in engineering and in science labs. Before earning a command, he spoke to astronauts who captained ships equipped with a gravity drive. Many remarked on the difficulty of describing how just beautiful it was when the engine engaged and the ship slipped into compressed space. It was not until he sat in the command chair that he realized the entire experience was indeed beyond words.

While serving as a science officer on an Inner System ship years ago, he had a chance to work on the command deck a few times as the engine engaged. Dai told his wife it was like watching a sunset in space, except there was no horizon line. But here, now, with a small crew of his own, the sight was even more impressive. His mind raced, thinking how he would describe it when he got home. The only sight he enjoyed more was the warm sunrise around his family cabin back in Kyoto, which had preoccupied his thoughts for most of the day.

A series of twenty-seven calculated jumps took them near Mars, Jupiter, and Saturn. Each time the system shut down and normal space faded into view, they were met with a new sight. McNair Station in orbit of Mars. The shiny network of domes and lights on the largest worlds of the asteroid belt. And Home Base Four, the new mega station under construction on the surface of Ganymede.

After moving past Saturn's orbit, the crew took time to rest, eat, and converse in the mess hall. It took nearly an hour and a half for a message to reach Earth from that distance, and another hour and a half for a reply. The messages to Home Base One tended to be long, so no details pertaining to the performance of the ship and crew went unsaid. The schedule allowed a solar day to pass before making the next set of jumps to the outermost planets.

Now back on the command desk, Dai's senior crew were at their stations, ready to go again.

"How do you feel, Captain?" Salah turned away from his consoles next to Dai. "Are we ready to proceed?"

Dai looked at the measurements coming in on his instruments. The display showed the distance between Earth and their current position.

"We have come so far." Dai whispered. He smiled, thinking how he would soon be back home with his family. His crew was not aware of his plans to retire early in another year. Soon he would have nothing more to do than to sit around that very old cabin. His children would soon be heading to university, and he wanted to spend as much time with them as possible.

"Begin countdown for the next burst."

2235

The alarms, gasps, and cries continued to echo in his head. Despite sitting alone in a small closet for almost five minutes, Gallus Winter could not seem to stop that blaring cacophony from ringing inside his ears.

The sound of the explosion coming in on the Home Base Two control room speakers rattled everyone on duty. The explosion came from the rear engine, ripping the ship apart like a zipper. The open comms channel to the world newsfeeds captured both the sound of tearing metal and every scream from the crew before they were claimed by the vacuum of space.

Any ship that was out on a mission in the solar system continuously fed information back to Earth for analysis in case of a system failure. In this instance, the ship was only ten light seconds away from the base. It would have been easy to troubleshoot most problems if there had been enough time. The chain of events that caused the explosion must have taken place in a few seconds. It was an unthinkable disaster in this era of spaceflight.

Gallus forced himself to stand up. He straightened his light gray shirt which bore his name and title of Chief Administrator of Home Base Two underneath the emblem of The Exchange.

He had barely been in the job for three weeks, and this latest mission to deliver parts and supplies to the station in orbit of Oberon was to be his unofficial welcome. Missions were running to the outer system twice a month, and it was as normal a routine as a run to the library. Having presided over the first loss of life in space in over two centuries was hardly how he imagined his tenure beginning.

Swallowing hard, Gallus took a step out the door of his office closet and into the front office area. A team of reporters was waiting outside his door for answers.

Twenty-two people were gone, and he had nothing to tell them.

Gallus walked past his desk and picked up his jacket. It nearly knocked over a small, framed drawing of his pet poodle, drawn by his son. He remembered the smile on the boy's face as he presented it to him for his new 'space office.' Gallus put on his jacket and walked over to open the door. The onslaught of questions from the press was immediate.

"Mr. Winter! What have you learned about what took place on board the *Tereshkova*?"

"Have you been in contact with the families of those on board?"

"Is there an official response from The Exchange Government, Mr. Winter?"

"Did you miss any warning signs? Was the *Tereshkova* in need of repairs?"

Gallus brushed though them. "We have no official statement yet. There is still a lot of data to comb through." He made his way down the sleek, empty hallway as the press corps stayed with him. "I'm on my way now to have a conversation with The Exchange Council, and I can assure you that all of us are just as eager to learn what happened to the crew up there as you are."

He walked through the door to the main control room, shutting it behind him and leaving the reporters outside. Technically it was a breach of protocol since members of the press were supposed to have total access to all main centers of activity on mission days. He guessed that under the circumstances no one would bother reminding him of it.

"Marcel, what do we have?" Gallus called out as he took his seat.

"The system is processing the data," the assessment officer said. "There was only a second between the emergency alarm and the start of a reactor breach. After that, the gravity drive went critical and exploded, consuming the ship."

Gallus struggled to hear over the buzzing room. "What was the reason for the alarm? What triggered it?"

"It looks like a failure in shielding and coolant around the reactor."

Gallus walked closer to Marcel's station, lowering his voice. "That can't happen."

"I know, Mr. Winter, but that is what it looks like to me. From here it is the only explanation that makes sense."

"Are you telling me we had a double failure on a ship that's not more than ten years old? Coolant systems and protective shielding, just switched off?" Gallus tried his best to keep his voice low, not wanting to cause any more panic than was already happening. He ran his dark fingers across his forehead, trying his best to breathe normally as a sinking feeling filled the pit of his stomach.

"Janiis, get me a secure line to the council, please?" Gallus said.

"Yes, sir! In your office."

Gallus pushed his way through the reporters, picking up the pace so he could get to his office and secure the door before they heard whom he was talking to. He removed his jacket once again and tossed it onto his reclining chair. A large square on the bright white wall next to his desk illuminated, allowing the video feed from The Exchange's ruling council chamber in Bern to appear.

"This is Gallus Winter. Thank you for taking my call." His eyes scanned the image on his wall. "Is the First Councilor not with you?"

"He is still on a call," said another member, whose thick New Zealand accent reminded Gallus of home. Gallus leaned against his desk as a representative from the Congo rose to speak.

"What do you think happened, Mr. Winter?"

"My team has informed me that a failure in the coolant and protective shielding led to a breach, which caused the gravity drive to overload and explode." Gallus' hands swished back and forth as he explained. "We do not yet know why the backup systems did not kick in, nor why the alarm was only trigged a second before the explosion."

The next question came from a councilor from Chile. "Do you have any theories?"

Gallus touched his index and middle finger to his lips before speaking. "I am hesitant to speculate without sufficient evidence."

"Indulge us, please."

"Well," Gallus breathed, "I have never heard of this level of system failure in an Outer System Ship, especially one this recently constructed." He swallowed hard before taking in a deep breath. "There are only two things I can think of. The first would be human error, either during a recent upgrade or during the mission."

"And what would the second be?" Another council member asked.

"The second would be deliberate sabotage."

The Council Chamber was suddenly awash in whispers, murmurs, and gasps of surprise. Gallus closed his eyes for a moment. It hurt him to think such a thing, much less say it out loud. He waited until the chamber calmed down. The representative from Chile spoke again.

"Bring us all the information you have. Be here tomorrow morning," he said before closing out the channel.

Gallus pivoted away from the wall as it faded back to opaque white. He looked down at his desk to see a dozen indicators on his comms panel blinking. A tear rolled down his cheek as he realized several of them were from family members of the crew of the *Tereshkova*.

***

Gallus sat on a bench outside the council chambers. The last time he visited the Capitol of The Exchange in Bern, Switzerland, was during his junior high school field trip. He had seen a dozen virtual tours of it since then, which hardly did the experience justice. It was an old building, dating back nearly three hundred years before The Exchange was organized into a global ruling entity.

A series of plaques lining the wall in front of him explained the brief history of the building, which was at one point called the Federal Palace. Each plaque was written in a different language, so that all who visited would be able to learn the history of the building and why it was chosen as the seat of power for the new government.

"Hello, Gallus."

Gallus looked up to see the face of First Councilor Dai Tanaka, head of The Exchange Government. In his early eighties now with silver hair, he smiled before sitting down on the bench.

"I love this hallway, don't you?" Dai said. "So much of our world is new and remade. It's refreshing to see a place with history, character, and flaws." He smiled as he spoke.

"First Councilor…" Gallus began to speak but was interrupted by a wave of Dai's hand.

"I'm here as your friend, Gallus."

"…Dai. I'm still at a loss about what happened to the crew of the *Tereshkova*."

Dai continued to look along the wall, which was adorned by dozens of paintings.

"Do you know the age of the youngest painting in the hallway?" Dai asked.

Gallus shook his head. "I'm afraid I don't."

"Nearly a century," Dai replied. "Do you know why?"

"Dai, if I could…"

"Humanity used to live for the arts, in one form or another. Over the past few hundred years, we have become a society of scientists and explorers. That's why I was tied up earlier when you called. I was talking to a group concerned about our dying interest in creative endeavors."

"I see artistic things all the time," Gallus said. "There were billboards along the street, ads at the transport terminal. Beautiful sidewalk murals outside the gardens.

"Over ninety percent of which are done with AIs. There are many who feel that our progress, our continuous reach into space, shoved aside other things we used to view as equally important. Children that used to be enamored with music, painting, and films are instead dreaming of physics and engineering. Ensuring that the growing amendments and exceptions to our artificial intelligence bans, and our own ambitions, do not stamp out our creative flame is what I thought the worst part of my week was going to be."

The First Councilor let out a long sigh before speaking again. "You, however, must feel like you are undergoing a true baptism by fire," Dai chuckled. "I do not envy you these next few days. It will be hard. But that is why you were recommended for the position. The council is confident in your ability to lead the investigation." The older man leaned closer. "You will find the answers, I'm sure."

"I don't know if I should be leading this effort." Gallus saw Dai's expression fall from one of sympathy and smiles to one of cautious anticipation. Gallus took a deep breath in before continuing. "I have been working at Home Base Two for not even a month and find myself overseeing the worst exploration disaster since the twenty-first century. If word gets out that we suspect an act of sabotage, it could cause a panic."

"So far, we are keeping it under wraps," Dai replied, smiling once again. "I trust your team to keep that information hidden from the public until we have a definitive answer. Members of the council will do the same."

"I am considering tendering my resignation, Dai."

Dai's expression changed again. He turned away, staring straight ahead. "Why?"

"I'm in over my head. I'm an engineer. A techie. I'm not an administrator."

"And yet, here you are."

"I don't know if I should be here," Gallus whispered.

"It only takes one broken piece for a tower to collapse," Dai said. He looked at Gallus once again. "The society you and I grew up in and take for granted was not won easily."

"My resignation from this position would not cause society to collapse, old friend."

"No, but you should be mindful of what it could do." Dai looked at a family posing for a picture near a statue down the hall. "You have not been in your position long, true. But you are there, and people are looking to you, for guidance and wisdom. Your sudden departure in the middle of a crisis like this would only leave people feeling worse."

Gallus shook his head. "Are you saying that I should stay just so members of my team don't panic?"

"No," Dai replied. "I am asking you to sit and think about the good you could do. Finding your footing while dealing with a catastrophe is not fair, I understand that. But you are capable, and that is why you're here."

Dai stood up. "The session will start in 10 minutes. I look forward to your report, my friend." He patted Gallus on the shoulder.

The First Councilor began walking down the long hallway. He paused after a few steps to turn around.

"I know what it's like to end up in a job you were not seeking. Please, take some time to think about it." He pivoted on his heel and continued walking, leaving Gallus alone on the bench.

***

Gallus walked up a single flight of stairs, eager to reach his hotel suite for the night. His report to the council went well, and he was given the go-ahead to lead a full-scale investigation that would include all personnel at Home Base Two, individuals in charge at the shipyard in Sacramento, and anyone who had worked on the *Tereshkova* during a system upgrade at McNair Station.

"Iced coffee, please," he asked the food sequencer. The machine embedded into the wall beeped obediently and began dispensing ice cubes and coffee into a cup. Saying please and thank you to household machines was not normal for most, but it was a habit by now. It was part of a multi-pronged strategy by he and his wife to teach their son about manners.

He grimaced after taking a sip and put the cup back into the machine. "Oat milk, please." The machine added a splash of oat milk, beeping again after completing the requested task. Gallus took out the cup and tasted it again.

Checking his wristcom, he decided it might be the perfect time to catch his son before school. Before he could make his way over to the comms panel, he heard a knock.

"Oh, for fuck's sake," Gallus said under his breath. He walked over to the door. Instead of an attendant with a set of fresh towels, he saw a tanned young woman with dark brown curly hair.

"Can I help you?" asked Gallus.

"Hello, Mr. Winter. My name is Charlotte Salazar. I have some updated information regarding your investigation. Marcel suggested I bring it to you as soon as possible." She held out a pair of data pads. The emblem on her jacket showed the seal of both Home Base Two and The Exchange, which was impossible to fabricate.

"Oh, sure. Come in," he said, leaving the door open. "Were you with the team that left with us this morning?"

"I was, yes," Charlotte said. She placed the pads on the table and stood in the middle of the room.

"You're in life sciences, right? Botany or something?" Gallus asked.

"Ecology," Charlotte said.

"Ecology, that's right! Sorry. I haven't had a chance to meet everyone face to face." He took another sip of his iced coffee.

"Well, it's nice to meet you, sir. Have a good night."

Gallus's brow furrowed as he watched the young woman close the suite door behind her. After another minute of finishing his iced coffee and listening to the occasional transport go by overhead, he walked over to a terminal and requested a link up to Home Base Two. The spread of personal home AI assistances had grown over the last century, but here in Bern, Switzerland, there was still some hesitancy to build them into the city's historic infrastructure.

"Please present clearance code," the computer said.

"Four one two, dash, three two alpha, dash, beta victor seven. Gallus Winter, requesting."

His home terminal appeared on the wall monitor as it would have in his office. He called up the file for Charlotte Salazar. Born in Providence twenty-seven years ago, she graduated from Harvard two years ago with a Master's in Ecology & Biodiversity. He stared straight ahead for a moment, wondering what it was that struck him so odd about this particular employee.

The nagging feeling continued as he talked to his wife and son, and then again after he ate a salad. After putting his dishes in the sanitizing unit, he pushed the button for the front desk on his terminal. The front desk attendant answered.

"Yes, Mr. Winter?"

"Is there a Charlotte Salazar staying here tonight?"

"One moment, please," she said. The seconds she took to look it up felt like an eternity. "No, Mr. Winter, there is no one here with that name."

"Okay, thank you." He closed the channel, attempting to make sense of all in his head. As far as he knew, everyone on his team was staying at the same hotel. There could have been a problem with a reservation, but he assumed he would have heard about it if members of his team had to go someplace else in the city.

Pacing around the room did not help much, but it was the only option currently available to him.

An hour later, he had something.

"Salazar. Salazar," he whispered, walking back over to the panel that was still hooked up to the Home

Base Two computer system. There was something about that name that continued to nag at him.

Typing in the name, Gallus asked the computer to cross-reference the name with files related to astronauts within the last two hundred years. Nothing. The next question pertained to anyone at the head of The Exchange, either elected or appointed. Nothing.

"What am I missing? C'mon, Winter, think..." Running his hands through his fine hair, he walked back and forth across the room again.

After ordering another iced coffee from the food sequencer, Gallus looked for references to other employees in Home Base Two. Nothing again.

"Okay, let's go back. How about Home Base One?" He waited as the computer displayed the name of Leandra Salazar, a public relations expert from Home Base One from 2104 to 2106. After that, she resigned to relative obscurity.

"But not just you..." He punched in another command and waited. The image of Martea Salazar appeared on her screen. "Martea Salazar. Served two presidential administrations over four years as press secretary and then a communications advisor. After which she resigned to focus on her personal life." He entered another command into the terminal as he whispered to himself, bringing all three women on the screen simultaneously.

"What the hell?" Gallus blinked. The facial features of all three women were nearly identical. A slight difference in the nose of one. A slightly smaller jaw in the other. But it was practically the same woman. Three faces, three different time periods.

"Who the hell are you?" he whispered.

"You can call me Charlotte," a voice from behind said. The surprise nearly startled the young administrator out of his shoes.

Gallus spun around to see Charlotte Salazar, standing there once again in the middle of his room.

There had been no creak of an opening door or the sound of footsteps on the old wooden floor. "How did you get in here?" he asked.

"I'm sorry for startling you," Charlotte said. She stood with her arms are her side. Her entire body was so motionless that it almost looked off, like his mind was having trouble accepting something so still.

"Who, or what are you?" Gallus asked, pointing to the pictures on his monitor.

Charlotte took a step toward the monitor. "Looking up my family history, I see."

"Those aren't you, are they?" Gallus replied. "Did you have yourself altered? If so, the surgeon did nice work. Very, very close."

"I've never had surgery, Mr. Winter."

"Well, there is no other explanation. No one would look that close so many generations apart." Turning back to the wall, he continued, "The difference is too similar even for the first two. Someone else might assume Martea was gifted with unusually strong genes, but not me. It's too bizarre."

"Please don't resign your position, Mr. Winter."

Gallus froze. "What did you say?"

"I asked you not to resign."

Only his wife, who was back in Sydney, and Dai Tanaka earlier today, knew that he was considering leaving his post. Neither would have a need to talk to a junior ecologist from his staff.

"How do you know that?" he asked.

"There's no simple answer to your question."

"Then I'll take a complex one."

"The Signalers are still out there, Mr. Winter."

Gallus backed up until his back hit the wall. "What?"

"The reason your people decided to reach deeper into space," Charlotte looked out his window. "You read about it as a child. The Seven Signal was received by your people in 2036."

"'Your people?'" Gallus tried his best to control his breathing. He turned around to look at the pictures again. *Three people from three different important eras of space exploration, all in relatively unimportant roles*, he thought to himself.

"You have good instincts," Charlotte said. "It's why you should not resign."

It was too fantastic. Gallus forced himself to take a deep breath before the vein throbbing in his temple became visible from across the room.

"Tell me what you want, what all this is about, or I am calling security," Callus growled.

"You are correct. I was there with the first Inner System test ship," Charlotte said. "But Martea was there in 2036. This is just a look we have appropriated several times since."

"What are you?"

"Someone who wants you to find them." She pointed out the window to the night sky.

"Who?" Gallus asked. "The Signalers?"

"Yes."

"Are you one of them?" Gallus asked.

"No. We come from much farther away." She walked over to the window. "We visit Earth from time to time to watch and observe. To guide. But never to influence directly."

"A guideline you seem to be breaking by telling me not to quit my job."

"It is a risk, you are correct. But it is one we now deem necessary."

Gallus looked out the window. The moon was high in the sky. With a good pair of binoculars, he could see the domes scattered across the surface. "Why?"

"Because they need you."

Gallus smiled. "They're still out there?" He looked out the window again. "We never knew. The signal lasted only a short time, and never repeated."

"They were calling out for help."

Gallus whipped around. "Help? W-what happened?"

Charlotte's expression changed to something akin to sadness. It was like she was wearing a mask that didn't quite fit her face. "Hundreds of years ago, we tried to contact them. We were alone in our area of the galaxy and sought out life that could understand us, and perhaps exist side-by-side as friends."

"What did you do? Did you send a ship to make contact? Land on their planet?" Gallus asked.

"In our normal state, we do not have a physical form – at least not in the way you're familiar with." She lifted her hand up in the air, looking at the fingers. "It can be done for a short amount of time, with great effort. But after a while, it becomes too taxing, and we must return to our natural state of existence."

"What happened between you and The Signalers?" Gallus sat down on a chair in the kitchen. His fingers tapped nervously on the chair leg, and he could feel his pulse drumming away in his temples.

"We attempted to reach out, consciousness to consciousness. But we had never talked to another sentient species before." She looked down as she spoke. "They were not able to recover from the initial encounter."

"Why? I don't understand. You seem to be doing fine with me."

"We did not appear physically to them when we tried to make contact. We tried to reach out with our consciousness." Charlotte took a deep breath in. "We were eager to reach out and explore, to learn more about the universe. But the species you call The Signalers, they exist in an almost totally empathetic state."

"Empathetic?" Gallus asked.

"Who you call the Signalers are connected as a species in a rather unique way," Charlotte explained. "My kind is capable of linking minds as a singular consciousness, but they were something we were not fully prepared for. They read and absorb everything–facial expressions, body language, what you might call 'energy.' It is all filtered into a total understanding of those they interact with. When we reached out telepathically to a small group of them, it caused shock, confusion, and fear. There was nothing visual for them to take in. They could not process an interaction the way they were used to doing so."

Gallus said nothing. It was all he could do at the moment to remain calm as he took it in.

"We had never attempted contact with another sentient species before," Charlotte continued. "It is why we appear to you in this manner now. Our experience with the Signalers taught us many painful lessons.

"You said they reacted with fear. What happened after?" Gallus asked.

"Those few reacted with fear and anger. It was read by a group of others and spread like fire across a dry brush. Or madness. Theirs was a society where feelings and empathy run so deep. Thousands of years of balance with their world and solar system were lost. It was horrid to watch as it burned through a society that was on the verge of leaving its home system, as yours is now."

Gallus sat, taking it all in. "So why are you here, helping us?"

"We prefer to think of ourselves as a silent guide. We do not force your actions, but we do provide the tools for the right messages to spread," Charlotte said. "Suggestions and influence, but never direct interference."

"A PR specialist..." Gallus whispered.

Charlotte nodded. "Yes. And there were other interactions you have yet to uncover."

"But how is it that you can just disappear each time? No one has ever thought to come looking for you?"

Before departing, we can leave a strong impression on everyone we have interacted with.

Gallus could not tell if the words were reverberating in the air, or just inside his mind. But her mouth was not moving.

We do not like to manipulate, as I said, but once our time is done at a critical juncture, we make sure no one that we have interacted with comes looking. Records remain, but no one typically has the urge to search. Obviously, we are not going to take such precautions with you.

"Okay. I guess I can buy that. But what about The Signalers? Are they still out there?" asked Gallus, pointing toward the window.

"Some, yes," Charlotte said, speaking aloud again. "But their cities were largely destroyed. Technology fell into disrepair as they quarreled with and murdered one another. Intelligent life is so rare in our galaxy, and the fact that we helped nearly destroy such a promising civilization is unbearable to my kind."

"I can't even begin to imagine."

"And we would not wish you to. But humans can help."

"How?" Gallus paused, swallowing hard. "Here you are, as impressive and capable as any lifeform I could imagine. If your species could have such a disastrous first contact, how can you be sure humans will succeed? You seemingly can probe and influence minds, while our best have never fully understood the contents of the Seven Signal."

"True understanding requires a conversation," Charlotte said. "You must first be able to talk to someone to grasp what they have to say. Over great distances and greater differences, signals and spacecrafts filled with information serve as little more than a greeting."

"I had a friend in college who was a top linguist. He too, said there was only so much we could learn without something more interactive. Used to joke he would give anything in the world just to have two hours to speak with one of the Signalers."

"You will see, soon. It will not be long until you have the means to reach them and show them a light they have not seen in years. You use facial expressions and gestural communication in ways beyond our ability. You also live your entire lives as physical entities, which we cannot do." Charlotte touched her face before continuing. "While humans do not experience empathy on the same scale, we believe you can connect with them."

"I'd like to think we're fairly empathetic. The Exchange developed an entire global economic system around empathy. Those who need help, medical care, food, and shelter, have all they need. Our means of producing surpluses have changed so much over the last century," Gallus said.

"This is true, but you also can look at someone who is angry, and not feel anger yourself. That is something The Signalers would have a great deal of difficulty with."

"I think I understand."

"Before their technological base collapsed, a few who remained unaffected put together a framework of their language and culture," Charlotte said.

"The Seven Signal!" Gallus exclaimed.

"They knew their society was collapsing. It was an attempt to let the universe know they were there. A last cry into the night for help." Charlotte's face twitched and winced as a look of fatigue began to set in.

"Not all children grow up, Mr. Winter. There have been many intelligent species in the galaxy. Too many over the eons perished before ever leaving the confines of their own solar system. Humanity has reached that point. You're ready to make the leap beyond the Sol system. And the Signalers are waiting for you." She winced again, leaning forward on the coffee table. "I have been in this form for three years. I'm tired."

"Is there anything I can do?" Gallus asked.

"Yes," Charlotte replied. "For a century, your progress into space has been about exploring. That is admirable. But your people long ago were able to calculate where the Seven Signal originated from."

"They suspect it came from Kepler-1649c".

Charlotte nodded. "Please don't let them forget."

"I won't." The young administrator ran his hands through his hair again. "It's going to take time to get back out there. I will need to find out the cause of the explosion, as you know."

The alien closed her eyes. Her brow furrowed as she concentrated. "You will find no malice."

"Are you saying it wasn't sabotage?"

"There will always be, as you call it, a human factor. This will always be risks, but you must not lose faith."

"So, something must've been missed during repairs," Gallus thought aloud. He rubbed his face before looking back up. "Thank you. You took a risk coming to me like this. I take it you don't want me to tell anyone about this conversation of ours?"

"I trust you to keep that information safe," Charlotte said with a wink. She mustered up the effort to straighten up. Gallus noticed that her skin began to shine brighter.

"Your species will make things right," she continued, "After the syzygy."

"After the syzygy? What? You mean like a planetary alignment?" Gallus asked.

"Nothing so literal," Charlotte answered. "When all things are as they should be and all the pieces are aligned, humans will make their next great leap."

Gallus squinted as he watched her writhe back and forth.

Please find them!

Those final words did not come from her mouth. Gallus simply heard them in his head again. He jumped back as her form dissolved into the air around it. All that was left was a dim white glow that slowly faded away.

Gallus stood motionless in his hotel room as his breath shuddered.

"We will," he whispered.

J.D. Sanderson

2389

First Councilor Enden Wallace stared out the window from his office in The Capitol of The Exchange. He wondered how many of his predecessors did the same thing before a big day. The view of historic Bern was beautiful and calming. It was the ideal scene to calm one's nerves.

Enden had served as a representative for a large district from the Northern American continent for twenty years, with five of those having been as First Councilor. With his term as leader of the governing body coming to an end, he was looking forward to going home to Halifax. While many of his contemporaries relished the idea of serving past their hundredth birthday, he was looking forward to retiring at the relatively young age of seventy-one.

A stack of paper-thin tablets continuously beckoned from the desk in the center of the room. One report detailed the construction of the new mental and emotional health center in Beijing, which would serve as a hub of research and development into the well-being of humans across the solar system. While initially receiving pushback from some of the other councilors, it was eventually passed with overwhelming support.

"If money is no longer a facet of human society, then neither should barriers to mental care," he said before putting the construction project up for a vote. "Just because we have wiped out hunger, supply chain shortages, and degenerative diseases, does not mean we still do not have work to do. There will always be people in need of help."

Under that report was the construction of two new bases; one on Callisto, and another in orbit of Triton. Once completed, there would be over two hundred separate colonies across the Sol System.

In his eyes, the only thing that came close to the mental health center in Beijing was the dedication and launch of a new class of exploratory vessels. Enden picked up the paper tablet, reviewing the design of the massive ship.

The rotating cone-shaped hull provided artificial gravity, just like in the Inner System and Outer System ships humanity used for hundreds of years. The engine that powered it, however, was something entirely new.

Enden's moment of relaxation was interrupted by a call.

"Forgive the interruption, First Councilor, but there is a message coming in from Luna."

"Thank you, Yara. Please put it through." Enden sat down in his chair as the holographic image of Danel Parra, chief administrator of the Luna Shipyard, was projected above his desk.

"Good morning, First Councilor," Danel said.

"Good morning to you as well, Danel," Enden said, looking again at the paper tablet detailing the new exploratory ship. "Is something wrong?"

"There has been an accident, First Councilor."

"An accident? Did something happen with the ship?"

"The ship is fine, but Captain Carden has been killed."

Enden closed his eyes as he took in the news. "How did it happen?"

Danel gestured with his hand to manipulate his holographic transmission. A copy of the medical report appeared alongside his image in front of Enden Wallace. "Captain Carden was visiting one of the labs in Anchorage with his engineering team. He fell off a ledge during an examination of some of the Folding Drive's testing components."

"He fell?"

"Yes, First Councilor. Almost six meters. He landed on his head, breaking his neck instantly." Danel tried his best to contain his emotions. "There was nothing the medical team could do."

Enden shook his head. With all of humanity's advancements, wiping out cancers, nervous system disorders, and psychological diseases, it was easy to forget that there were some things medical science could not fix.

"Has his wife been notified?" Enden asked.

"Not yet. This happened only a few hours ago," Danel said. "I was about to make the call myself.

"Thank you," Enden said. "But I will take care of it. Please forward me a copy of the report."

"Of course, First Councilor."

"I realize this is not nearly as important right now as the passing of a colleague, but I assume you will see to a replacement for him on the mission?"

"Yes. I will have made my selection by tomorrow."

"Very good. Thank you!" Enden closed out the transmission, taking a deep breath in before paging his assistant. "Yara, I need a biographical file on Captain Rili Carden."

"Of course, First Councilor."

The information appeared on his holographic display. Rili Carden was forty-four, married, and a father to four children. His wife, Olean, was a botanist and agricultural advisor to several large farms in the midwestern region of the United States.

Enden initiated the call to Olean, clearing the mist out of his eyes before it connected.

***

Danel Parra adjusted his Zero-G harness. Like many orbital platforms and habitats across the system, Elpis Station spun to simulate gravity. Its three separate rings spun at separate velocities in order to achieve one Earth G. Travel between the three different rings required moving through small corridors that went from the outermost ring down to the central core.

Moving from one ring to another sometimes resulted in a bit of dizziness due to the different rotational speeds. The harness kept someone moving at a steady pace to avoid any such discomfort.

Once he was safely inside, he made his way down the curved hallway toward the primary docking hatch. The main viewing port gave an excellent look of the *Hypatia*.

The white and silver hull glistened against the docking floodlights. Danel always swelled with pride when he saw blue, white, and silver logo of The Exchange next to the ship registry on the hull.

"Mr. Parra!"

"Doctor, hello!" Danel shook the chief medical officer's hand. "Did the provisions and equipment on board the *Hypatia* meet your expectations?"

"They did," Doctor Asher Stein said. "I just came back from bringing a few extra things on board. Emiry told me if I tried to bring one more box on board, we'd have to install some additional bulkheads."

"Is she still on the ship?" Danel asked.

"Emiry? No. She said she was heading down to get something to eat in the galley."

"Good, I need to talk to her."

"Is it about Rili?"

"In a way," Danel said. "I spoke with First Councilor Enden Wallace again this morning. We've decided to give Emiry command of the *Hypatia*."

Asher stared at his chief administrator for a long moment before looking down at the floor. "You think that's a good idea?"

"She's more than qualified for the position, Asher."

"Rili had commanded two other ships before being selected for the *Hypatia*," Asher said. "He commanded the mission to Proxima Centauri two years ago through multiple bursts. Emiry is a good officer, but this is a deep space mission. I don't need to tell you that we have never gone this far out."

"I understand your hesitancy, Asher. But I believe she will make a fine captain."

"Oh, I agree, for a normal mission, yes but, sometimes I wonder…" Asher trailed off for a moment.

"What about?"

"If she has the stomach for it."

"Stomach?"

"I mean no disrespect to her, Danel. She's a wonderful person and highly skilled. But she can be a bit, well, it's hard to describe."

"She cares. Deeply. She has a connection with everyone. It's a quality we've put at the top of our lists for mission commander candidates for decades."

"I know." Asher nodded in agreement. "I guess it will take some time to get used to the idea of someone other than Rili commanding the mission."

"Rili led with his guts in training, but he also understood when to lead with his heart," Danel said. "Emiry is the same way."

"I can't argue with you there."

"She has the perfect combination of intelligence, bravery, scientific curiosity, artistic imagination, and empathy. If she hadn't spent so much time preparing for this mission, I can tell you for certain she would have been assigned to command another ship by now."

"Really? I hadn't heard that."

"Emiry isn't one to boast, but you can trust me. I was the one who offered the ship to her."

"Alright, my friend." Asher held his hands up. "You've sold me. And I'll do my best to make sure everything goes well on the mission. Speaking of which, are we keeping our launch date?"

"No, the Council has agreed to postpone for a few weeks. They understand what a strain this has put on the crew."

"Strain is an understatement. Most of us worked with Rili for almost two years."

"That's another reason why I'm choosing Emiry," Danel explained. "She worked alongside Rili every minute of those two years. She probably knows the ship better than the designers do."

Asher shook his head. "No doubt. There wasn't a single space or corridor the two of them did not crawl through together. Who is going to take over her duties as the executive officer?"

"I was thinking of Amandi. He can handle navigation and executive officer duties simultaneously, I believe. And it would be better to keep it simple than to introduce another office the crew has not worked with."

"I agree," Asher said. "I've got to go down to the medical storage room and see if there's anything else I can sneak on board."

Danel laughed as he slapped Asher on the back. Proceeding once again down the curved hallway, he opened the door to the galley to find Emiry sitting alone at a table, reading a book as she ate.

"Am I interrupting?" he asked.

"Hello!" The young officer stood up. "Please, sir. Join me!"

"Thank you," Danel said. "I'm sorry to bother you while you're relaxing. I wanted to discuss the Kepler mission.'

"The crew is a mess," Emiry said. "I directed them to the counselor's offices, here and on the lunar surface. Gave them as much time as they need."

"Are they taking your advice?" Danel asked.

"Some are. Others might not be ready to grieve yet. It happened so fast. None of us even got a chance to say goodbye to Rili. He wasn't just our commanding officer, sir. He was our friend."

A gentle smile made its way across Danel's face. "Glad to see you're following protocol."

"It's more than protocol," Emiry muttered, "I'm married. I have a shoulder to lean on. Most of this crew have dedicated their lives to a mission like this. They need someone to talk to."

"Have you told your Kaati yet?"

"I did. She was devastated, like all of us," Emiry said, running her hands through her hair. "I still can't believe it myself."

Danel paused to thank a young kitchen aid who brought him his usual cup of tea. He looked back to Emiry as she put the cover back on her meal. "I'm giving you command of the *Hypatia*, Emiry. Effective immediately."

Emiry slowly put her food container down. Her eyes shifted up while the rest of her face remained pointed at the table.

"Me?"

"Yes, you."

"I'm sorry." Emiry fidgeted with her utensil for a moment as she took his words in. "It's barely been two days since…"

"I understand, and the mission will be delayed. I'm not asking anyone to jump into the saddle immediately. But I am asking the officer who knows this new ship and her crew better than anyone else to take command." He stood up.

Emiry nodded. "This wasn't how I wanted to take command of a ship."

"No one would, and I know you had your heart set on seeing this mission through with your friend. You even passed up a command of another ship last year to stay on board."

Emiry nodded.

"First Councilor Wallace and I are confident in this decision," Danel said. "I've got to get back to my office. I will send a message out to the crew shortly." He pushed his chair in. "Congratulations, Captain Adin."

***

Captain Emiry Adin looked to her command crew. They were together again for the first time since the funeral two weeks earlier on Earth. The day after the memorial, she took them out to one of their favorite restaurants, like she and Rili had done dozens of times before. What she anticipated would be a nerve-wracking night went better than she could have guessed.

Personal experience taught her there was always a bit of apprehension when someone new took command. Thankfully, by the end of their meal, the crew was smiling again, talking eagerly about the Kepler mission.

Emiry looked over her shoulder and nodded to Danel before speaking.

"We launch tomorrow," Emiry announced. "Like you, I still find myself thinking about our friend, Rili. We would all have him back in a heartbeat if we could. Like him, I'm confident in each and every one of you. We've all worked together, side-by-side, for over two years. There is no finer group in The Exchange. And if there is anything I can do to help you on this mission, please let me help you, no matter what it is."

"We know you will," said Amandi Renna, who yesterday accepted the promotion to executive officer.

The rest nodded in agreement.

Danel nodded from the back of the room, clearing his throat before stepping forward. "I know you all will make us proud." He pointed to the panel where he could operate a holographic display. "I'd love to try and say something smart and poignant, but lucky for you there are far better people out there suited to such things."

The group laughed along as he activated the panel and called up a projection. Everyone seated around the table straightened up as the image of First Councilor Enden Wallace.

"I'm sorry for surprising you all like this, but under the circumstances, I thought an intimate address would be more appropriate."

The crew exchanged glances as Enden continued.

"Your crew, your ship, is the culmination of something started generations ago during one of the most tumultuous periods in our history. We learned for the first time that we were not alone in the universe. A signal from outside our solar system planted the seeds of hope that we as a people so desperately needed."

Emiry smiled.

"I am so proud of what we have accomplished. For over three centuries we have grown as a people and culture. At the same time, we have strived to learn about a culture completely alien from our own. What we know about them has only continued to pique our curiosity over the years."

"Their vocalizations remind us of stringed instruments, and their artwork evokes emotions like ours. They could project radio waves into space, but we do not know if they ever left their own planet. Did they survive? Are they still waiting? We do not know, but we are going to try and seek answers. They reached out with a message announcing themselves to the galaxy. Now it's time for us to answer."

The First Councilor looked around the table at each member of the crew. "Engineer Dalis Ritten, Doctor Asher Stein, Lifesciences Specialist Yensin Chen, Executive Officer Amandi Renna, and Captain Emiry Adin. Our hopes and dreams rest with you and the *Hypatia*."

"Thank you, First Councilor," Emiry said.

"In light of the recent tragedy, I suggested to Danel that we suspend the usual pomp and circumstance that would normally accompany such a prestigious launch," Enden said. "So instead, I will simply say good luck to all of you. I hope you find us the answers we as a people have searched so very long for."

***

Emiry strapped herself into the command chair as the *Hypatia* rose above the ecliptic. An hour ago, she went into the private communications chamber for a discussion with Kaati. Over the decades, it became a tradition for all Exchange explorers before making a long-distance trip. The preparation for faster-than-light jumps took several hours, and people were encouraged to put that time to use with something relaxing, enjoyable, or a trip to the communications chamber. Despite trying her best to keep it together, Emiry could not stop herself from shedding a few tears as her wife wished her luck.

Amandi placed his hand on his captain's shoulder, offering a sad smile.

"Did you say goodbye to your son?" Emiry asked.

"I did. Told him to be brave and watch out for his mother and grandparents." Amandi took out a small sheet of paper he brought out from the chamber. "He sent me this to synthesize out and put at my station."

Emiry's big smile glowed as she looked at a family portrait consisting of Amandi, his wife, son, both sets of grandparents, and their pet cat. She marveled at how beautifully the colors flowed from one end of the drawing to the other.

"Does he like his new school?"

"He does! We couldn't believe he was one of the first accepted to the Academy for Creative Arts' new campus in Okinawa." Amandi smiled, remembering the pride he felt two months ago when he told the crew his ten-year-old would study at the prestigious school. The first campus opened twenty years earlier in Manhattan. Its popularity led to a boom in the fields of music, art, and writing, which in turn led to the need for a second facility. "He's going to do great things."

"I'm sure he will."

"He is going to study with one of the original three instructors," Amandi said with a grin.

"Really? I didn't know any of them were still teaching there!" Emiry said. "That is incredible! My nephew hopes to be accepted soon to their writing program."

They were interrupted by a tone filling the bridge, indicating that calculations were complete. During trial runs, the ships new Folding Drive took Emiry, Rili, and the testing crew from one end of the solar system to the other in a matter of minutes. This mission would take them farther than anyone had ever gone.

"What do you say, Amandi? Should we test her under full power?" Emiry asked.

"I believe we are ready," Amandi replied.

"Enter coordinates for the first burst," Emiry ordered.

"Entering now." Amandi punched them into the navigational computer. "Folding Drive is coming online. How does it look, Dalis?"

"Two minutes to full power," Dalis answered.

"All hands, strap in," Emiry said.

The front section of the *Hypatia* ceased rotation, cutting off the artificial gravity. The rear section of the ship containing the Folding Drive locked in as a faint blue glow came from the exhaust slits.

"Monitoring shows green across the board for all personnel," Doctor Stein announced.

"Ships functions are blue," Yensin added. "Everything looks perfect."

"We're at your command, Captain," Amandi said.

Emiry clicked a communication relay on the console next to her chair. "This is the *Hypatia*. We are green across the board and ready to commence engine ignition."

"Glad to hear it, Captain. Safe travels. We'll be waiting," Danel replied.

Emiry opened the internal comms channel. "All hands, strap in. We are locking the command section." The hull echoed as the rotating nose of the ship locked into place, ceasing the artificial gravity. Amandi chuckled as a few of the others scrambled to buckle themselves in.

Emiry leaned forward after the locking sequence finished. "Activate Folding Drive."

***

The *Hypatia* emerged out of its final burst, slowing down four Earth Astronomical Units from Kepler-1649. The glow of faster-than-light travel was replaced by the soft glow of the red dwarf star. Captain Adin and her crew released their seating restraints as the drive section disengaged and the command section began to rotate again.

Emiry and Amandi stood at the front of the ship as they approached their target planet of Kepler-1649c. The near-earth-sized planet orbited its mother star at a distance of six million miles.

"There it is," Emiry whispered, pointing to the second planet. Next to the enhanced image on the main monitor was a digital layout of the Kepler-1649 system; A small sun and two planets.

"It's beautiful," Amandi whispered. "Well worth ten days of jumps."

Emiry looked back. "Lifesciences?"

Yensin's eyes widened as the data flowed into her monitors. "I'm reading an atmosphere. Median temperature is a bit cooler than Earth's, but it's comfortable enough for liquid water on most of the surface. Gravity is approximately 1.07 Earth G's."

"Thank you, Yensin," Emiry said. "Amandi, please bring us into orbit."

"Yes, Captain," Amandi said.

"What about technology?" Emiry asked. "Are we getting any signals? Broadcasts?"

"Nothing yet," Amandi said. "Imaging shows what looks like the remains of multiple structures in large areas, but there's no way to know how old they may be. They look like cities from here."

Emiry and Amandi exchanged glances. Words were not necessary. The thought was obvious. Three hundred and sixty-six years after the signal was received, and almost seven hundred and sixty-seven years since it was first sent, the *Hypatia* and her crew may have been too late to ever meet who sent it into space.

"Let's suit up."

***

The *Hypatia* was equipped with two small auxiliary craft, designed to enter a planetary atmosphere. Each held several days' worth of food, oxygen, and medical supplies. Blunt and compact, they attached to the underside of the drive section toward the rear of the ship.

With assistance from a few of their crewmates, Emiry and Amandi were fastened into their atmospheric suits. Now seated inside the cramped landing craft, they signaled the command deck of their intent to leave the ship.

"Atmosphere does not appear to be as thick as home." Yensin's voice came through clearly into their helmets. "I think you can expect a relatively smooth descent."

"Thank you, Yensin. Course is plotted for one of the larger city areas. This is Captain Adin, detaching."

The miniature craft released from the hull of the *Hypatia*, tumbling at first in the blackness of space until Emiry and Amandi initiated the stabilizing thrusters. Once attitude control had been regained, Amandi began moving them closer to the planet. Emiry looked over at her executive officer as he mumbled something under his breath.

"What's that you're whispering?" she asked.

"A traditional Kenyan prayer my mother taught me," Amandi replied. "Passed down through the generations."

"All this time and I never knew you were spiritual."

"It's a personal thing to me. I know many are not, so I never wish to appear imposing."

The craft rocked back and forth, sending them reeling and straining against their chair restraints.

"What the hell was that?" Emiry yelled. Three of the cockpit's alert lights came on.

"I don't know. Something hit one of our thrusters. The second engine is damaged."

"What hit us? Did the cameras catch it?"

"Something, I don't know. Might have been some kind of animal."

"An avian species?"

"I don't know," Amandi said with increased tension in his voice. "But we're going to have to land soon."

"I think I can get us to the outer part of the target area," Emiry said, straining to adjust the controls. "If you want to say any more of those prayers, I would appreciate it!"

Emiry used what thrusters were left to stabilize the ship as it descended rapidly toward what looked like the ruins of a large city. The landing craft slammed into the ground, jostling its passengers back and forth in their seats as it skidded to a halt against a large, dilapidated structure.

***

Amandi opened his eyes, trying his best to tune out the blaring of the craft's emergency alarms. He looked around to make sure the hull was secure before grabbing and shaking Emiry by the shoulder.

"Captain, are you alright?"

Emiry lifted her head up, touching her palm to the side of her helmet. "I think so. Come on, let's get up and see what kind of mess we're in." She undid her straps and stood up, taking the time to make sure she was steady on her feet.

"Should we radio the *Hypatia*?"

"We will soon. They probably monitored our descent. If they saw what happened, they will probably send down the second landing ship soon. Before we contact them, I need to know *what* to tell them," Emiry said. She reached over and opened the side hatch, revealing a landscape of red, tan, and violet hues. It blended beautifully with the blue and violet sky.

The pair made their way to the rear of the craft. One of the four engine ports appeared to have cracked open. The impact against the old building smashed the side of the craft. Steam was venting from within.

"Oh no," Amandi said.

"What is it?" Emiry asked, coming around to look with him.

"The reactor. I believe we are leaking a small amount of radiation."

"Toxic?"

"Not enough to get through our suits. We could shut it down entirely and contain it, but the ship won't take off again. We should be…Wait! What is that?" He turned to look behind another building.

"I heard it too," Emiry said. "Sound like a small rock falling."

"Sidearm, captain?"

"No, not yet," she ordered, motioning for her executive officer to follow her slowly around the corner of the building. They looked around, seeing nothing that could have caused the sound moments ago.

Emiry looked up to the sky to see a small, winged animal diving to the ground. It disappeared behind a building.

"Maybe that's one of the things that did us in," Amandi said. "If it hit a vent…"

They looked around again, still hearing a faint scraping sound. Emiry grabbed Amandi's hand while putting her finger up to her lips. Her exec nodded.

Moving slowly, they crept back around the old building they walked from a few moments earlier. They looked at one another as the sound of something scraping on metal entered their headsets.

"Slowly," Emiry whispered. She peered around the corner just enough to see a small animal putting a limb on the side of their landing craft. "Oh, my God…"

"What is it?"

"Amandi," she whispered. "It's…"

The silhouette was one that every school child on Earth had learned about for over three and a half centuries. It stood nimbly on four limbs. Two more protruded from what could be called shoulder and chest region. On the top of its body at the front, there was a protrusion that might have been a head.

"Amandi…"

"We did it, Emiry," he replied, trying to keep his voice low. "It's them!"

"I know! I can't believe it!"

They watched as the brown, wolf-sized alien touched the small ship. It lifted an arm, touching the cracked part of the engine with six multi-segmented digits. Three were at the front of the arm and three where a human thumb would be.

The feeling of awe quickly dissipated as the small creature seemed to reel back from the ship. They watched silently as its two grasping limbs touched the sides of its head.

"Emiry, what is it doing?" Amandi asked.

Emiry watched in total silence; afraid any sudden movement might cause it to take off running. Before she could decide what to do first, the creature emitted a low, cello-type vocalization. It swelled and dipped, changing pitches like a stringed instrument with no frets.

As it turned around in their direction, it became apparent there was a single large black mass on the front of the head that looked almost like the compound eye of an insect. No mouth, ears, or nose was apparent. Its skin looked like it would feel like that of a dolphin or orca, with small white spots across most of the back and legs.

It backed away from the ship slowly, continuing its vocalizations. The head mound shook back and forth, while the skin around the ocular mass flexed around in all directions.

"Emiry. The radiation," Amandi whispered.

Emiry gasped. The creature was wearing no suit, no clothes. Without a detailed analysis, there was no way to guess what even a small amount of radiation from their craft would have on an alien creature.

Unfortunately, the effect was becoming clear.

"Do you think we can help?" Amandi asked.

"I don't know," Emiry breathed, "but we have to try. This would not be happening to it we hadn't crashed here. I'm going to try and approach it."

As she stepped forward, Emiry's boot landed a small batch of pebbles. Similar in consistency to Earth shale, the stone crumbled underneath her. The small alien's body bowed in the middle to look at what had caused the noise.

Emiry held up her hands. "It's okay," she whispered.

The creature writhed again, shaking its head while trying to keep its balance on wobbly legs. The low cello-like pitch it emitted previously now shot up to something more akin to a screaming violin. Amandi winced as the sound rang in his ears.

The creature backed up until it hit a wall. The hind legs gave out, and it fell back. The human explorers watched helplessly as it tried its best to stabilize itself with its front two legs and arms. Emiry's eyes closed as the tone changed to something softer. It took all her will not to look away.

"What can we do?" Amandi asked.

Emiry watched the creature as it jerked and shuffled on the ground. Its feet had six appendages that looked like a cross between hooves and claws. The digits moved individually like twitching human fingers. They scraped against the dust, revealing an artificial surface underneath.

Emiry and Amandi were standing on an old, worn road.

Looking around, it became apparent they were standing in the middle of what was once a large city. None of the buildings reached more than two stories, but imaging from orbit showed an organized area larger than Nairobi.

Emiry brushed her hand against the wall of a building. It chipped against her hands, one of the many signs the buildings were neglected for centuries.

"What the hell happened to them?" Emiry whispered. "How did they go from sending advanced interstellar signals to this?"

The captain touched a control on her wrist panel, removing all tint from the glass of her helmet. Something told her it needed to see her face.

"Hello," she said, taking a step forward. She raised her hands in the air, showing her palms to the injured alien. "It's okay."

"It's not going to understand us," Amandi called out.

"I know. But maybe it understands more than we think it does."

Together they walked to within ten feet of the creature, which still was crying out in soft, mournful bursts of sustained sounds. Amandi followed her example, removing the tint from his helmet.

The small alien shifted its head-like mound, so the dark eye patch met their gaze. It looked at Emiry, then at Amandi.

Emiry's heart broke. She took two more steps forward before dropping to one knee. Amandi took another step forward, crouching down.

"It's staring at us," he said.

"Yes. It's stopped vocalizing."

"Maybe it is too weak?"

"Maybe," Emiry replied. "Or maybe it's something else."

The muscles around the little alien's eye patch moved, changing its shape into something wider. Amandi smiled and nodded as he leaned closer. The alien's skin rubbed against the ground as it shifted position. A tiny amount of the skin's outer layer flaked off.

Amandi and Emiry looked at one another before turning back to the hapless being.

"I am sorry this happened," Amandi said, sounding like a parent talking to a child.

"We came here to meet you. To thank you for inspiring us. We never wanted to hurt you," Emiry added. She maintained eye contact with the creature as a tear rolled down her cheek.

The skin around the eye patch flexed again as it emitted a small, violin-like tone. Amandi's expression broke down as he fought back tears. The frightened creature let out more gentle singing sounds. Its expression changed again as it stared at both human faces in front of it.

The alien shuffled forward a few inches, trying to muster up strength from its hind legs.

"It's okay," Emiry nodded. "Yes…" She put her palms up, reaching out to it.

It took another step forward, looking again at both of their faces. Amandi nodded his head with a sad smile.

Two of its four legs gave out as it tried to take another step forward. Amandi rushed forward, lifting the alien into his arms. The longer fingers on its front appendages stretched out and contracted rapidly.

"Take it away from the engine," Emiry yelled. She ran up to the craft and opened the main hatch. Entering her command codes, she deactivated the reactor and shut it down, grounding the ship permanently. She sealed off the engine and closed off the reactor valves, hoping it would contain the leak.

Emiry rushed over to Amandi after exiting the craft. He was still holding the creature after carrying it down the unkempt road to a safer distance.

"It just keeps staring at me."

"Maybe that's how they talk," Emiry said. "Similar to sign language maybe?"

She reached down to touch the side of its head. The black and speckled eye patch changed shape again.

"I'm sorry," she murmured, trying to contain her emotions.

A loud, singing pitch rang out from behind them. It twisted in the air from a clear note to the sound of rubber being dragged across a piano wire. Amandi gestured with his head for Emiry to turn around.

Four more aliens appeared from around a nearby building. They moved silently and gracefully, exchanging looks with one another. A second vocalization appeared to their left, as a fifth alien moved around from the wreckage of what might have been a craft or vehicle. The metal casing showed signs of exposure and rust.

"What should we do?" Amandi asked.

Emiry looked around as the aliens continued to cautiously approach. She touched the face of the injured one in Amandi's arms. It lifted its head and looked to the group of four, who were now only several yards away.

"Look!" Amandi exclaimed.

The four aliens locked in on the injured one's face, stopping only to exchange glances with one another. Amandi and Emiry looked on in silence as the facial muscles around the large eye patches moved around. After another minute, the aliens all began to emit low vocalizations, filling the air like a musical chord.

Emiry let out a small, joyful gasp as another tear ran down her cheek. She looked down to see their injured friend continue to sing to the other aliens. It glanced back and forth between them and its own kind. She found it difficult not to be moved by the musical exchanges filling her ears.

The song was unlike anything even the most advanced recreations would have guessed. In the centuries since the Seven Signal was first heard and recorded, many had attempted to recreate the sounds, hoping to understand how the song-like language worked. Hearing it now, Emiry and Amandi realized just how much there was to learn about them.

"Do you think they know we're not trying to hurt them?" Amandi asked. More singing came from around the buildings.

Above the buildings, they could see the arc of the *Hypatia's* second landing craft coming down. Emiry and Amandi exchanged a quick glance, happy to see help on the way.

The small alien reached out with one of its two forelimbs and pointed three digits toward the sky. It then pointed to Emiry and Amandi. The vocalizations continued as it reached back to the sky again.

"I think they know." Emiry smiled down at their injured friend. She leaned down, stared at the black eye patch, and whispered. "We heard you."

After the Syzygy

//I⅃IC\I/U:I⅄

"They have made contact."

"Impressive."

"Yes, it is."

"It was witnessed by our watchers."

"Events conducted by physical entities rarely seem to go as planned. Nevertheless, this one seems to have yielded a positive outcome."

"There is so little data to go on."

"Agreed, this is only the second physical species we have seen achieve this level of technical proficiency."

"You are forgetting the Hathnrea."

"They exterminated themselves before they could even leave the confines of their atmosphere. An incredible waste of potential."

"Yes, it was."

"It is a miracle the Sivenen also did not go extinct."

"Do you think the humans will be able to assist them?"

"Unknown. The damage inflicted to their society was beyond anything we could have imagined."

"The humans possess both ingenuity and patience."

"And empathy."

"Empathy, yes. A key component for working to help the Sivenen."

"It must be asked – what exactly do we expect the humans to do? They have made contact, yes, but they may not be able to provide what is needed. Their craft are designed for short-term exploration, not for the long-term technical assistance the Sivenen require."

"That is true. They could not have anticipated the needs of the situation."

"I too am concerned."

"We could continue to guide the humans further."

"Indirect contact?"

"Yes, indirect contact may be necessary."

"A new human likeness would need to be appropriated for that."

"It has not been done since our sole direct contact with humans."

"Gallus Winter."

"Many of their years have passed. There was no indication he told anyone of his encounter with you."

"I did not remove impressions of me after our discussion. To do so would have undermined the entire reason for direct contact."

"Additional indirect contact, influence, with the humans may be necessary to fully undo our mistake with the Sivenen."

"There may be no way to fully undo such a mistake."

"I believe that is correct. There is no way to restore their civilization to the power it was. They have lost contact with their colonies within their star system."

"Very few remain alive on the moons."

"The madness spread to the entire population."

"Restoration is impossible. Healing is not."

"Humans may not yet be capable of providing that."

"We do not know yet."

"What was the last status of the first direct contact between the humans and the Sivenen?"

"The captain of their ship stayed on the surface for two planetary rotations. She then boarded one of the auxiliary craft and returned to her ship. Our watchers indicated she plans to return for the human who remained on the planet."

"Amandi Renna."

"It could be dozens of rotations before he is rejoined by other humans."

"They left him with provisions. He will survive."

"He must have stayed behind to establish relations with the Sivenen."

"I believe it is more basic than that."

"How so?"

"During my time on Earth, I witnessed their compulsion to help those in need."

"You reported it changed their entire system of government."

"Over the years, yes. I believe this human stayed behind to evaluate and learn more about the Sivenen species. The signal from the Sivenen brought the human population out from the edge of a potential dark age. That is something they as a people have not forgotten."

"Still, I believe we should make direct contact with the humans again. Encourage them to continue."

"I agree. In time our three races could work together."

"What about the others?"

"The higher ones."

"It's not proven they even exist."

"What about them?"

"Contact was never proven."

"I believe direct contact was attempted by them."

"Who else could have made the changes we witnessed over time?"

"You are assuming the humans could not have made the change on their own?"

"Not in so short a time, no."

"Do we tell the humans about our suspicions?"

"No."

"Not yet."

"We must first establish the higher ones exist. And if proven, establish their intentions."

"The Humans and Sivenen must be warned if their intentions are hostile."

"There is no proof of hostility."

"If a fourth race does exist, we must contact them."

"I agree. Intelligent life is so rare in our galaxy. Perhaps in our universe. We must attempt contact and learn all we can."

"Perhaps they do not share the urge to contact others that we share with the humans and Sivenen?"

"Curiosity is inherent to all intelligent lifeforms, regardless of form. I believe they will be open to contact with us if we find a way to make it possible."

"I agree."

"As do I."

"We will concentrate efforts on discovering the truth about the higher ones."

"What about the Sivenen?"

"Humans will do everything they can to help them. While their biological differences may be too great to supply food and medicine directly, they will use all the technical skill at their disposal to help."

"It is true, they have an innate ability to adapt to new circumstances and challenges.

"What if a large portion of them do not agree to help? There are over thirty billion of them across their solar system. How can we be sure they will agree to help an alien species?"

"I stayed with them many times over the centuries. I am sure."

End of Part II

About the Author

J.D. Sanderson lives with his wife, daughter, and mini poodle in South Dakota. A lifelong fan of science fiction, J.D. published his first book in 2018. His previous works include A Footstep Echo, The Clock's Knell, and Around the Dark Dial. When he's not writing, you'll find him watching a science fiction movie, reading a good book, and enjoying time with his family. Follow him on Twitter @ascifiwriter

Acknowledgements

Thank you, Joanne, for once again doing everything you can to help me get to this point. My stories are always better after your help, and your encouraging words mean the world to me. Thank you to everyone who has taken the time to read my books. I hope you find this one as enjoyable as the rest!

Printed in Great Britain
by Amazon

37488467R00065